T0065242

Legends of the Thunderbolts:

EXODUS PROTOCOL

KENDALL KNIGHTEN

authorHOUSE®

AuthorHouse™
1663 Liberty Drive
Bloomington, IN 47403
www.authorhouse.com
Phone: 1 (800) 839-8640

Published by AuthorHouse   2/15/2018

ISBN: 978-1-5462-2981-0 (sc)
ISBN: 978-1-5462-2980-3 (e)

Print information available on the last page.

TABLE OF CONTENTS

Chapter I   Choose 1
Chapter II   Ashes to Ashes 14
Chapter III   The New Reality 22
Chapter IV   Fool's Errand 30
Chapter V   The Grand Escape 42
Chapter VI   The Grand Exodus 57
Chapter VII   Cruel World 68
Chapter VIII   The Unexpected 84
Chapter IX   Lack of Humanity 92
Chapter X   A Second Chance 102
Chapter XI   Do-or-Die 112
Chapter XII   Changing the Tide 134

CHAPTER 1

Choose

Earth was once a beautiful world. It used to be a world with vast skies, fresh air, lush trees, refreshing waters, lively cities, and a diverse population of seven billion humans. But, Earth had many chapters and legends in its story that made it a world of Wolves in Sheep's clothing; and then, the war began. A war between the Onyx[1] and the Legion[2] was one that has permanently changed the world. Before it all, Earth was a beautiful planet in the cosmos, renowned across the Universe for its beauty and a world with so much life inside of it. Now, the Earth has skies blocked by black, sick clouds, ashes falling like darkened snow, tainted air and trees, waters mixed with blood, cities turned into barren wastelands destroyed by the apocalypse, and the population lives in fear as it has been dwindling to a small fraction; billions have lost their lives in the carnage. The Earth has been transformed into a shadow of its former self; a world of chaos and fear and where peace and happiness has nearly died. The war is reaching its end with the Legion reigning over the world. Cities fly the banner of the Legion; Onyx bases and settlements have been destroyed; and Onyx soldiers are either killed, imprisoned, or scattered in the winds.

Inside of Mundi Castle[3] under a massive thunderstorm, Legion soldiers are armed in Ultranian technology, marching across the city, searching the town for Onyx spies and undercover soldiers who will

---

[1] An organization that was built to insure peace and order in the world.

[2] An order made of super-powered Deities, the world's deadliest assassins, Gang leaders, mad scientists, and interstellar, extraterrestrial war-race called the Ultranians. Known to the masses as the New World Order.

[3] The ancient and once sacred castle city turned into the Capital of the Legion.

interfere with the grand event. The castle itself is so heavily-guarded and so well-protected, there is nothing on Earth that will get near the city by force. If a force were to enter the castle, they will not reach or leave the castle alive. The castle's newly installed helipad, bearing the Legion symbol instead of the traditional "H", has Legion heavy-gunners standing guard in case the prisoner attempts to escape. These soldiers greet a Legion-Ultranian Prisoner Transport, landing on its thrusters with the capacity of carrying five prisoners, but it is carrying only two prisoners. The hatch of the transport opens and Gordon Foreman[4] and Omegatronus[5] walk out on to the helipad. A captain approaches Gordon and gives him a military greeting.

Legion Captain: Apex-General.

Gordon: Status report, Captain.

Legion Captain: We have completely secured the city. The castle's defenses are at full-strength. No force in this universe can get inside or out the castle without our say-so. We are still working on the interior repairs.

Gordon: We can never be too sure, Captain. Omegatronus, take to the skies. Make sure there's no possible threat to the castle. We do not need any more unwanted guests breaking inside the castle.

Omegatronus: Yes, Apex-General.

Omegatronus activates his propulsion systems and takes off, soaring in the air in search for any spies.

Gordon (to the prison guards): Bring out the prisoners, NOW!

Prison-Guard: You two shrimps heard the Apex-General. Move it!

---

[4] The Legion's highest ranking General. Veteran turned feared crime-boss. The Apex-General. Caucasian. White hair. Blue Right Eye. Left Deadeye. Large scar running through left eye. American. Age 30.

[5] Elite Ultranian battle android with enough fire power to destroy any army in any environment, even armies in the void of space.

The prison guards are escorting the two prisoners outside of the transport. These two prisoners are Tom Sullivan[6] and Jamie Kelly[7]. They have been beaten, captured, and stripped of their weapons and equipment. Tom has a large black eye on his right eye and Jamie has bruises and dried blood stains on her face. They are wearing nothing but old, gray, worn-out prisoner uniforms with old worn-out shoes, and have Ultranian hand-cuffs for their wrists and Ultranian shackles for their ankles to bind their hands and feet to make sure they cannot escape. Jamie, because she was born with a human-monkey tail and she uses it like an extra limb, has her tail cuffed to her neck. Gordon stops the escort in order to look Tom in his good eye. Gordon, through eye movements, orders the Warden to make Tom and Jamie get on their hands and knees. The Warden presses the command on his prison-gauntlet that is synchronized to Tom and Jamie handcuff and has the cuffs fall to the ground on their hands and knees, the Bowing-Mode. Gordon stands over Tom as Tom looks up with disdain.

Gordon: Well, well… this is the highly feared Tom Sullivan, leader of the notorious Thunderbolts.
Tom (disdainful): I guess our fame proceeds us for the Apex-General to know who we are.
Gordon: Funny. This is the last day of your miserable lives as child-soldiers. Any final requests before you get put out of your misery?
Tom: Yeah… How about you go fuck yourself, Foreman?

Gordon punches Tom in the face so hard, a tooth and blood flies out of his mouth.

Jamie: Captain!

---

[6] Leader of the highest-ranking elite Special Forces unit, the Thunderbolts. A soldier trained in the ways of the Onyx ever since childhood. Caucasian. Blond hair. Straight Hair. Blue eyes. American. Age 19.
[7] The most highly-skilled Scout of the Thunderbolts. The Animal Spirit Host of the Monkey Spirit. Well known for her monkey tail. Caucasian. Red hair/tail. Long hair. Amber eyes. Canadian. Age 19.

Gordon kicks Tom in the stomach, dealing a large amount of damage due to him wearing Ultranian armor made of Ultranian metal alloys and Tom is exposed to the force of the metal alloys that is a thousand times stronger than New Magnesium Alloy. Gordon grabs Tom by his hair and picks his head up. Jamie wants to help Tom, but a Legion Prison Guard puts his gun to the back of her head in order to restrain Jamie.

Legion Guard: Any sudden moves and your dead.
Gordon: Wow, you still have some fight in you. We'll see just how much fight is left before you break. Warden, get them on their feet.

The Warden takes the hand-cuffs off of Bowing-mode, allowing Tom and Jamie to stand up.

Gordon: Let's go.

Gordon leads the escort inside the castle; the guards push Tom and Jamie forward to get them to walk.

Mundi castle is an ancient fortress. Inside, it contains medieval suits of armor, ancient swords, shields, and spears displayed on the walls. Painting hang in all of the hallways of knights, sorcerers, assassins, kings, and queens dating back eras before the city of Eridu was established, and recently installed Legion technology floods the halls of the castle.

As they walk through the halls of the castle, Jamie sees that the interior has taken massive damage; she sees holes in the walls and the ceiling, damaged pillars, destroyed Ultranian defense guns, and shattered armor displays. She has no idea what happened inside the castle; Gordon and Tom, on the other hand, know who attacked the castle.

Jamie (worried, whispers): I got a bad feeling about this, Captain.
Tom (calmly whispering): Don't lose your nerve, Jamie.
Jamie (desperate): Please tell me you have a plan, Captain. You always have a plan.

Tom: Just keep your cool. An opportunity will come…
Gordon: Quiet, prisoners!

Tom and Jamie go silent for a brief moment.

Jamie: Tell me, Apex-General. What happened in here? It looks like a tornado with a wrecking ball tore through here.
Gordon (Sense of superiority): Now why would I tell you that, Circus-Freak?
Jamie: I'm just asking seeing as how we do not have not have that time left. You already plan to kill us, so maybe you can tell us before we die.

Gordon, being a strong believer of final requests before death, decides to talk.

Gordon: I will say this; what happened here gave the Dark-Knighten motivation.
Jamie: Motivation for what?
Gordon: You'll see soon enough.

Gordon opens the door to the Mundi Castle throne room, which is a large room with damaged and remains of pillars and a massive carpet leading to a broken throne. They look forward and they see Dark-Knighten[8] sitting on the broken throne. Gordon stops the escort in front of the steps to the throne.

Gordon: On your knees.

Tom and Jamie do not move. Gordon looks at the Warden and the Warden activates the Bowing-mode for Tom and Jamie's handcuffs and shackles to make them bow.

---

[8] The Supreme Leader of the Legion. Number 13. Multi-Racial. Light skinned. Shaved afro. Black hair. Hell Red right eye. Brown right eye. Freckles all over body. Body riddled with scars. Infernian-Sons Symbol cattle-branded on his left cheek. American. Age 19.

Gordon: Dark-Knighten, I have the special delivery for you.

Dark-Knighten, knowing what Gordon means by "special delivery," takes a deep breath with his eyes closed after thinking of what he had to do and why he had to do it. He steps out of the shadows, revealing his battle-worn Hell-Deity themed Ultranian armor. Jamie sees that Dark-Knighten looks exactly like Kendall Knighten Jr[9], not remembering that Kendall told her that he and the Dark-Knighten are twins and Kendall is only two minutes older. Dark-Knighten looks at Tom and Jamie and is not impressed.

Dark-Knighten (to Tom): So... These are the well-renowned Thunderbolts. I've been hearing time and time again that the Thunderbolts are the deadliest fighters in the Onyx, some of the most highly trained soldiers in the world. But looking at you now, I'm a tad disappointed. I was expecting someone older, like G.I. Joe. Not someone who I could've gone to Kindergarten with.

Tom: I can say the same thing about you.

Dark-Knighten: <Smirk> I can only guess that you've seen the castle and you know what has happened here..., what I was forced to do.

Tom: A Thunderbolt volunteered to be part of a mission to kill you and the Thunderbolt failed to do so.

Dark-Knighten: Do you even know who that Thunderbolt was?

Tom: Of course I do... Kendall Knighten...

Dark-Knighten, in a sudden bid blind rage with fire in his eyes, punches Tom in the Solar Plexus. Tom gasps in pain and leans forward from reflexes, putting his forehead on the ground. Dark-Knighten puts his foot on the back of Tom's head. Everyone, even Gordon, was caught off-guard with that burst of rage.

Jamie: Captain!

---

[9] Thunderbolt Field Operative. Abnormally powerful Knighten with an unstable energy-core. Multi-Racial. Light Skinned. Shaved afro. Black hair. Brown eyes. Freckles all over body. American. Age 19.

Dark-Knighten (pure rage, clouded mind): Bingo, we have a winner! Kendall Knighten! Kendall Storm Knighten Jr. was his name, the name of my brother!

Dark-Knighten grabs Tom by the neck and lefts him up in the air despite the handcuffs and shackles binding him to the ground. The rage balled up by Dark-Knighten is leaking out and he loses all of his composure.

Dark-Knighten (angry): You Onyx indoctrinated Kendall…, manipulated him, turned him into a lap dog. He came here wanting to kill me. I had to kill him. I had to watch him die. I watched as he faded away into nothingness…. He meant everything to me, the one and only person that I knew I could trust with my life in this world, the one person who was supposed to free me from the hell that *they* put me in so long ago! Now he's dead! He wouldn't be dead right now if it wasn't for you Onyx. He would still be alive if it wasn't for you Onyx!

Jamie, wanting to help Tom, makes a slight movement as she helplessly sees Tom get beaten.

Dark-Knighten: Gordon, control your prisoner!

Gordon kicks Jamie in the back, causing her to fall face first to the ground. He grabs Jamie by her hair, pulls her back to her knees, and puts his Ultranian revolver to her lower jaw. Dark-Knighten drop Tom and let him drop to the ground and puts his foot in Tom's head and presses down. Tom feels the pressure from Dark-Knighten's foot on his head.

Tom: He…wasn't indoctrinated. He came here to… save you. His biggest… intent… was to save you. We couldn't stop him from coming here… He would've give anything if it meant saving you.

Dark-Knighten takes his foot off of Tom's head as if he scrubbing dirt off his boots like a doormat and then takes a deep breathe in order to calm himself and get himself back into balance. Dark-Knighten looks at Gordon and Gordon lets Jamie go.

Dark-Knighten (calmed): I should kill you right now what happened here. But, I'm not, not right now anyway.

Tom: What's stopping you? Why not just kill us now?

Dark-Knighten holds his right hand in the air and snaps his fingers. Legion soldiers step out of the shadows of the throne room, three on the left side of the throne room and three on the right side. Each of the soldiers has a prisoner; the left side has Onyx soldiers, representing the entire Onyx army, and the right side has a man, a woman, and a pregnant woman who were fighting as members of the Resistance group who want both Onyx and Legion called "The League."

Dark-Knighten: Because you are going to choose…Surrender or Die. But, before you answer, you should know that you are not just answering for the rest of the Onyx, but for all the people of Earth who would choose to stand against us. Live or die.

Tom knows that his answers will have the hostages die, but he also knows that he cannot back down from the creed of the Onyx. He and Jamie decide to put their hands on their knees and take a deep breath to cool their minds as they close their eyes in unison.

Tom: If you truly know what an Onyx was, you would know what my answer is. You would know that an Onyx would never surrender to the lights of you.

Onyx prisoner: That's right, Thunderbolts. You can kill us right now, but you'll never completely defeat the Onyx. The Onyx will live on Forever.

Dark-Knighten quickly conjures up EC[10] dual-wielding, Dark-Chaos powered semi-automatic shotguns and instantly shots the Onyx prisoner in the head, blowing his brains out and splattering blood and organs on the Legion soldiers holding the prisoners. The prisoner's body fall forward and blood is flowing out of the body, resembling a river. The other prisoners are scared and are freaking out thinking that they may be next. Jamie tries her best to keep her eyes closed while Tom uses his years of practice to take a deep breath to not break.

Gordon: Damn.
Dark-Knighten: You have this confused. I don't have to kill you. All I have to do is show the world the truth.
Tom: What truth?
Dark-Knighten: You Onyx are not invincible. You Onyx are no saviors.

Dark-Knighten takes his shotguns and guns down the Onyx prisoners, aiming for their chests. The power of the shotguns was enough to completely scatter the body part that comes into the contact with the blasts. Small splatters of blood soar across the throne room and on everyone in the room. Gordon flinches as blood pellet hit his face; Jamie opens her eyes when she feels the blood hit her face; Tom keeps his eye shut and takes one deep breath for every gunshot.

Jamie: You bastard! Stop!
Tom (whispers): Jamie!
Dark-Knighten: You made your choice, Thunderbolt. This is the consequence. So I'll stop when all of you are dead, bitch!

Dark-Knighten turns his attention to the rebellious civilians; Jamie sees that Tom still has his eyes closed and is calm, but she does not see is Tom has conflict in his mind. He can tell that the civilians are the only ones left.

Tom: This is senseless carnage. It didn't have to come to this.

---

[10] Energy Core. The essence of every single human on existence.

Dark-Knighten: This is what you choose, Sullivan. Choosing to be defiant to the end. Now I said that you were choosing not just the Onyx, but for all of the people who would stand against the Legion.

Jamie: Dark-Knighten, this is between the Legion and the Onyx. Leave them out of this!

Dark-Knighten: This is between the Legion and the those who stand in our way. These fools made their choices too. And now, this is where their choices got them.

Dark-Knighten watches as the civilians are fearful for their lives, panicking and begging for their lives, but he feels completely nothing for them. He, feeling nothing but hate after what e had to do, effortlessly aims for the head of the man as tears flow out of his eyes like a river and fires, blowing the man's head into pieces. The women scream in utter fear as they watch the lifeless and headless body of the man fall on the floor. Dark-Knighten shots the woman in the chest to kill her instantly.

Tom: You're a monster!

Jamie (fearful rage): This is going too far!

Dark-Knighten (indifferent): You know… If I still an ounce of my humanity inside of me, then I would most certainly agree with you.

The pregnant woman, with her arms on her stomach, thinking about her unborn-child, is kneeing in horror as Dark-Knighten stands before her. She feels completely helpless as she thinks that Dark-Knighten will kill her and her baby.

The Pregnant Woman (begging): Please. Don't kill me. I beg of you. My baby. Please spare my baby. PLEASE!!!

Dark-Knighten puts the barrel of his gun in the woman's stomach, where the un-born child is supposed to be. Without anyone seeing, Dark-Knighten's eyes change purple and the pregnant woman's eyes change purple without her knowing. She can feel something inside of her.

Jamie: Don't do it!

Dark-Knighten: But, the thing is… My humanity was stolen from me… a long time ago.

Dark-Knighten pulls the trigger and fires a shoot that is less powerful blast to send the woman on her back. Jamie is in a state of horror and Tom finally opens his good eye as Dark-Knighten just kill unarmed, defenseless civilians and even an unborn child in cold-blood. Tom leans on his hands and puts his forehead on the floor, believing that this is his fault. Jamie is consumed in an anger fueled by fear.

Jamie (angry): You bastard! You cold-hearted, merciless bastard!!! You're going to pay for this! I swear, YOU WILL PAY!!!

Dark-Knighten redirects his attention to Tom and Jamie and walks in towards them. As he is walking towards them, he drops his E.C. ammo clips and conjures darkness-powered E.C. clips. He stands over the two and then turns his attention to Jamie and shots Jamie in the solar-plexus with a blast dialed down to not kill her, only to render her unconscious. Jamie grunts in pain before she loses consciousness as she falls to the ground. Tom quickly saw Dark-Knighten shot Jamie and he tries to crawl to her, but he is stopped by the handcuffs and shackles. He begins to think that one of his closest friends died and he did nothing about and can do nothing about it. Dark-Knighten puts the barrel of one of his shotguns in front of his solar-plexus.

Tom: Even if you kill us here, Dark-Knighten. Someone will stop you and the Legion.

Dark-Knighten shots Tom in his solar-plexus with the same type of blast that Jamie took and watches Tom fight to stay conscious. Dark-Knighten throws his guns on the floor to make them dissipate, gets on one knee, grabs Tom by his hair, and to hold him up to look into his eye; Tom is slipping from more damage to his body.

Dark-Knighten: Death is merely the angel of mercy in this world. You should know by now: There are fates worse than death.

Dark-Knighten watches Tom's face as he falls forward to the ground as he loses consciousness. He looks down on Tom and Jamie as they lie on the ground unconscious and near-death. He redirects his attention to pregnant woman and walks over to her. As he stands in front of her, he sticks his hand out and a light-blue light aura appears around his hand, the aura of his power of light. He uses his power of light to heal the Pregnant Woman of any damage she has taken. She opens her eyes, not knowing that she is still alive. When she realizes she is still alive, she quickly places her hands on her stomach to feel if the baby is still alive. Dark-Knighten slowly places his hand on her stomach to drop the Barrier of Darkness he placed around the unborn child to protect it from any damage. He looks into the Pregnant Woman's eyes as they return to her original state.

Dark-Knighten: Be glad you didn't have this child, otherwise you would be dead like the rest of them. Get her out of here.

Two of the Legion soldiers inside of the throne pick the woman up and they take out of the room; Dark-Knighten watches them careful escort her away. He then turns his attention to the Tom and Jamie and sees Gordon stare at him.

Dark-Knighten: What?
Gordon (surprised): You… spared the child.
Dark-Knighten: Gordon, use your head. Why would I kill an unborn child that hasn't even experienced life?

Gordon pauses as he cannot find an answer.

Dark-Knighten: Exactly… Now, get these two to the dungeon.
Gordon: But, why not just kill them now, Dark-Knighten?
Dark-Knighten (irritated): Gordon, are you questioning me right now?

Gordon (fearful): No, sir.

Dark-Knighten: Good. Now, get these two to the dungeon. I have
important business to tend to. They better be here when I get back.

Gordon: Yes, Dark-Knighten.

Dark-Knighten creates a large portal of ***Pure-Darkness*** that leads
into another realm of existence and steps through the portal as it closes.

Gordon (to the guards): Get these two to the dungeons, now.

Guards (in unison) Yes sir. Apex-General sir.

The guards form the prison escort take Tom and Jamie outside of
the Throne-room. Gordon watches the guards take Tom and Jamie.
He then looks at what is left of the throne and begins to think about
Dark-Knighten entering the Legion and then looks at it with disdain,
what he secretly feels about Dark-Knighten.

Chapter II
Ashes to Ashes

As the early phases of the war went on, the two warring factions have matched each other blow for blow; eventually the tide has turned in favor of the Legion, resulting in the Legion's total occupation of the planet. Onyx bases are destroyed, most of the Onyx's secrets are in the hands of the Legion, and Onyx soldiers across the planet are either dead, imprisoned waiting for torture and/or execution, or scattered across the planet with no leadership. Even the very symbol of the Onyx, their capital city of Magnus[11] was destroyed by the Legion's orbital Ultranian satellite lasers. The power of the lasers has reduced the city into ruins. Buildings have been destroyed; the very ground across the ruins has cracked open from the impact; and ash clouds cover the ruins and ashes are pouring down resembling the Winter of Death. Legion soldiers, heavily armed along with Ultranian hover-cycles, fighter-jets, and tanks, are searching for survivors to terminate on site as they march through the streets.

However, what they do not realize is they are being watched by Onyx-Grade security drone hovering over the Magnus-Ruins. Thunderbolt Antonio Turbo[12] equipped in an Onyx stealth suit with a signal shielder to prevent the Legion from detecting his signal, a long-distance Environmental-Scanner accessory in his helmet, and grappling hook gauntlet accessories on his arms for his stealth suit in

---

[11] The symbol of the proud Onyx. A city with four districts: The North is Shinto (the Military district), The South is Aurora (the Industrial district), the East is Olympus (the Scientific-Engineering district), and the West is Jacinto (the Academy district).
[12] Thunderbolt field-operative. Fourth oldest in the Turbo family. Terra-Deity. African-American. Braids. Black Hair. Brown eyes. American. Age 19.

order to maneuver across the ruins. Antonio is watching the surveillance feed alongside Generalissimo Richard Sullivan[13] using a surveillance computer.

Richard: Alright, the drone's live and we've got a clear feed.
Antonio: You call this clear, commander? I can't even see that much with the ashes. The city's ashier than I am when I run out of lotion.
Richard: I didn't need to know that? We need to send this probe to the Shinto-Tower.
Antonio: That was where the satellite laser impacted, Commander. I only got you out like seconds before the laser hit the ground. Shinto-Tower ought to be a smoking crater in the ground.
Richard: We'll never know for certain unless we...

The Drone's signal instantly cuts off as the drone has been shot down by an Legion Sniper. The computer displays on the screen, "Feed: Terminated. Surveillance Drone: Destroyed."

Richard: Dammit... change in plans. You'll have to go to the Plaza and check for yourself.
Antonio: Just one slight problem. I will need my powers in order to even get close to that crater and I cannot use my powers in this stealth suit.
Richard: It's the only thing that we have to shield our signal. So you will just have to make due with that.
Antonio: If I had my powers, I'll be able to sneak through the city no problem. But, they may be able to detect my presence even with stealth-suit.
Richard: You'll have to stay out their detection range. Onyx-Level can shield your signal, provided you don't detected. We're wasting time, they're marching for the tower now. Get going.

---

[13] The Highest Ranking leader of the Onyx army. Father-figure to Tom Sullivan. Caucasian. Light-Blond hair. Blue eyes. Straight hair. Age 55.

Richard gives Antonio high-power Ultranian pistols with armor piercing rounds and silencers on each.

Antonio: What am supposed to do with these?
Richard: Use them… It's all we have. Now go.
Antonio: Yes sir.

Antonio quickly converts his suit into it's stealth-mode in the form of a belt buckle and uses his Terra-Swim[14] ability and resurface above the ground. When he resurfaces, he quickly presses the converter on his belt buckle to activate the suit's battle mode. He can hear a oncoming patrol of Legion soldiers that detected the seismic activity left behind by Antonio; he grapples to a destroyed building to sneak away before they detect him. He reaches the top of the building he was after making his way up a large amount of stairs.

Antonio: Okay… I'm in a desolate city with ash falling like snow. I have to hide from this massive-ass Legion army that will kill me on sight. And I have to go to what is more likely a smoking crater in the ground, all in a suit that's blocking my Terra[15] powers, squeezing my nuts, and giving me a wedgie. And even with these guns, I can't fight back if I get caught. This is Bullshit.

Antonio checks his grappling hooks, limbers up by stretching his arms and legs, walks back for a running start, gets into a running position, turns on his Environmental Scanner to see his surrounding though the ash-infested winds obscuring his vision. He takes off to the edge and jumps off the building. He then uses his grappling hooks in order to maneuver through the city. Antonio is staying on the rooftops in order to keep from being seen from by the Legion and Ultranian soldiers and also staying in the vast shadows of the dark ruins to hide from the Legion's Ultranian jets. As he makes his way through the ruins

---

[14] Antonio's Terra ability to go underground and travel through the crest and mantle of the Earth like a fish swims in water.
[15] The ability to manipulate the Earth.

of the city, Antonio begins to wonder of all of his fellow Thunderbolts, especially Thunderbolt Bridgette Swanson[16] as she was the last person he saw before he went to save Richard from being destroyed along with the rest of the city. He eventually reaches a building in Shinto that gives him a visual and what he sees completely shocks him; he contact Richard.

Antonio (surprised): Uhh… Commander…, I have a visual on Shinto-Tower.
Richard: What's the status on the tower?
Antonio: That's just it; there is no tower. There's nothing left of the tower; it's a smoking crater in the ground. I said that this would be the worse case scenario too, Shinto-Tower was where the laser impacted. It's no surprise that the Shinto-Tower is nothing but a crater.
Richard: Do you see an elevator shaft inside the crater?

Antonio uses the zoom in his Environmental Scanner to analyze the crater. His scanner detects an opening inside the crater.

Antonio: Uhh… A-Affirmative.
Richard (relieved): <Sigh of relief> Good, a lucky break. Go inside of the shaft and into the bunker.
Antonio: What are you talking about a bunker?
Richard: I'll explain when you get down there. Time is wasting. Hurry.

Communication is shut off.

Antonio: This is not how I wanting to spend this week. Running around in a post-apocalyptic hellhole with ash everywhere and Legion soldiers out to kill my ass. Come to think of it, it's no different from growing up in the slums of Kinto[17].

---

[16] Thunderbolt Intelligence Officer. Feared by enemies and allies alike. Trained in the academy along side Tom. Confined to a wheelchair. Caucasian. Brunette. Brown eyes. Shoulder length hair. Glasses. Little freckles on upper part of her cheeks. English. Age 19.
[17] The Hometown of the Turbos and Gordon.

Antonio gets ready to jump off of the building, before he jumps, he hears a Legion fighter-jet flying behind him. He then thinks to himself, he can get to the crater faster via ship and he would look more like a badass while doing it. But, he sees that there are many Legion soldiers around the crater. He cannot think of a way to enter the elevator shaft. But, the deafening silence get struck when he hears a massive explosion in Shinto District. The explosion is so massive, Antonio thought it looked like mushroom cloud like Hiroshima in the WWII documentaries that he always feel asleep on. Legion Soldiers all across the city are scrambling as if they are under attack. Antonio sees another building on the other side of the crater light up before exploding, causing another explosion. Debris is flying across the crater; Antonio even ducks behind cover to keep debris from smacking into his face. Legion Soldiers in the crater are falling back from the chaos as they believe that they are under attack. The buildings left and right of the crater explode as well, causing more and more chaos. Antonio sees that there is an opening to enter the crater's elevator shaft, but he also notices that the building he's on is beginning to glow.

Antonio (irritated): Oh fuck my life!

He hears an Ultranian ship approaching; he jumps off the building without a second though and fires his grapple to attach to the ship. The building he was on explodes and shockwave blows Antonio back, causing the grappling-hook to be severed from the ship. Antonio plummet down to the crater; he quickly recovers and grapples to the shaft and goes straight to and down the shaft. He slides down with his hands and feet dug into the metal wall as he descends down the wall. He eventually stops before he lands on the destroyed elevator; he slips and fall on his butt while he was one foot from the air. He starts heavily breathing as he get exhausted from all of the adrenaline of the explosions as he gets an incoming transmission from Richard.

Richard: Antonio, I'm hearing explosions. What's going on up there?

Antonio (exhausted): I have no idea, commander. A bunch of building blew up around the crater and I practically got blown into the shaft down the crater.

Richard: Are you alright?

Antonio: I'm fine, Commander. What am I looking for?

Antonio pries open the elevator door inside of the damaged bunker on the other side.

Richard: Look for a silver briefcase. That is our only means of survival.

Antonio looks around the room where he would eventually see dead body in the room and he instantly moves away from it out of fight-or-flight reflex.

Antonio (scared): Oh shit!

He notices that something is shining under it and makes out that it is the briefcase, but he knows he'll have to move the body to get it.

Antonio: This is Fuckshit.

Antonio slowly moves towards the body, not wanting to touch it. Antonio flips the body with his foot picks it up by the handle.

Antonio: Okay, I'm starting to get tired of this shit. All this ash and dust. Where does all of this come from anyway?

Antonio contacts Richard to give him an update.

Antonio: Commander, I found the briefcase.

Richard: Good. Now bring it back to me. And whatever you do, do not engage in combat with the briefcase near. We cannot risk damaging it.

Antonio: Yes sir. I'll be in touch.

Antonio deactivates his communicator.

Antonio: Man, if I'd knew that he would be running around in some God-Forsaken city with motherfuckers out to shoot my black-ass into tiny piece with these alien guns, I would've just left his old-ass. I used to get enough ducking and dodging back in Kinto from the damned gang-bangers.

Antonio looks for a way to escape and figures out how to escape. He converts his suit into its stealth mode to channel his Terra powers in his hands and throw a couple of quick jabs at the steel wall, creating a massive dent. Antonio then kisses his finger tips, rams his fingers though the wall, and pierces through the wall and tears open a hole to the crest big enough for him to fit through. Antonio grabs the briefcase, then uses Terra-Swim out in order to escape the bunker.

Moments later, Richard is attempting to contact Antonio, but receiving no answer.

Richard: Agent Turbo come in. Agent Turbo come in. Report soldier.

Commander Sullivan hears a bang, a hole being blown in the side of the burrow. Richard pulls out his pistol thinking that the burrow has been compromised, but he lowers it when he sees Antonio walk inside.

Antonio: I can't answer my communicator if I'm underground, man. My hands were full as is.

He gives Richard the briefcase and the stealth-suit converter.

Antonio: Thought you might want that back.
Sullivan: Excellent work, Agent.

Antonio watches Richard open the briefcase to see for what he had to risk his life and sees that there is a computer inside it, not knowing that this is the Emergency Onyx Matrix (E.O.M) or what is does even if he heard of the name.

Antonio: What is that?

Richard: This is our last chance to turn this war around in our favor. I just have to contact the High-Council. With any luck, I should be able to contact them with this briefcase so they can initiate the evacuation protocol.

Antonio: "Evacuation Protocol?" So we can get out of this bit- Uh... I mean... place.

Richard: Yes... but it's going to take me a while. Just take five for now. I'll let you know if I need you to do anything else.

Antonio collapses on the ground from the none-stop running around the Magnus-Ruins and falls sound-asleep instantly. As Richard watches Antonio fall asleep, he instantly thinks of how Tom used to fall asleep like that as a kid after training.

Richard (worried): <Sigh> I can only hope Tom is still out there alive and well. The entire Onyx army is going to need him now more than ever. God knows I need him.

Chapter III
The New Reality

All of Earth's cities, especially the well known and heavily populated cities such as New York City, Tokyo, London, Paris, Berlin, Moscow, Mexico City, Beijing, Istanbul, and Sao Paulo, have been turned into desolate ruins. As a result, the Legion has built large military metropolises in a week across the world rather than rebuilding what the war has destroyed. Only populated by Legion soldiers and High-Ranking Officials, these large metropolises are so heavily armed with Ultranian weaponry, entire armies would get destroyed attempting to infiltrate them. All of these cities are also equipped with planetary guns with enough range to reach the moon and powerful enough to destroy objects even larger than Earth with a single barrage from one Legion-City. In addition, these cities are also built to survey entire countries to keep an eye on the remaining populace to snuff out any form of rebellion they can find.

With militarized cities across the globe, the Legion established and sustained its control over the planet with little to no resistance to their rule. This power would lead to a sense of superiority, leading to a special division of Legion soldiers called the Peacekeepers[18] going to the ruined cities and take everything from the population that survived the war and send it all to the military cities, leaving the people to fend for themselves.

---

[18] The division of Legion Soldiers that are built to preserve order in the Legion-occupied Earth, snuff out and destroy any and every form of rebellion, and to provide supplies for themselves and Legion soldiers by going into the ruined cities and steal any and every resources from the people.

Located in the Denver-Ruins, the sound of motorcycles tear through the silence of the desolate city as the Road-Vipers[19] ride through the ruined streets. Some bikers are riding down the streets with standard Earth firearms, observing the damage done by the war. Other bikers are walking through the desolate streets with hazard masks and hoodies while searching for one woman. The Peacekeepers and Road-Vipers are plundering the neighborhoods, stealing from the surviving masses and leaving them all to die. The Newly-Made Road-Viper Leader, Rattlesnake, contacts his biker who are searching for Bethlehem Khat[20]. Rattlesnake is inside of a Legion Settlement in the middle of the Denver-Ruins kissing up to the Peacekeeper captains to earn a place in the Legion.

Rattlesnake: Cobra, is Beth found yet?
Cobra: No. She's completely gone. Maybe she left the city. Maybe even the state.
Rattlesnake: No… she's still here in Denver. I know Beth. She would not run like a bitch. Keep searching, these captains told me that if we find her, we'll be in the Legion for sure.
Cobra: Oh hohohohohoho yeah.
Rattlesnake: Now hurry up and find her.

The Road-Viper start cheering for themselves as they continue their search for Beth on their bikes and on the ground.
Meanwhile with Beth, she rides through the highways from Denver to Aurora on an E.C. conjured[21] motorcycle. She is wearing a Road-Viper black and green wastelander suit, a biker suit with fibers to protect

---

[19] The deadly street gang that ride the streets of Colorado that is determined to rid Colorado of all gangs. They act as vigilantes, "Riding down the highway to Justice."
[20] The Titanoboa. Born with green skin, super strength, and super durability. Latina. Green hair. Shoulder length hair. Green eyes. American. Age 19.
[21] E.C. Construct: A technique used by the Safe-Guardian order. Allows a Safe-Guardian to conjure any weapon with their energy. From swords to guns. These weapons would be five to ten times stronger and more efficient than its actual weapon counterpart, depending on the skill of the user. For the highly skilled, vehicles can be conjured like weapons.

the wearer from radiation and a toxicity mask to keep from breathing in the ashes and a hoodie over the mask. Beth is riding with Kylie Shulls[22] holding on her. Kylie is equipped in her damaged Ultranian-Class Onyx battle armor equipped with a Velocity-Boots accessory, a Shockwave gauntlet accessory on her right arm, and a Shadow-Cloak gauntlet on her left hand. Beth is racing through Aurora as she is furious and Kylie is holding on for dear life to not fall with wind in his face. Kylie conjures a Tele-Link[23] for Beth to hear her.

Kylie: Beth, you're going too fast.

Beth: I can't fucking believe this shit! Those Sons of Bitches fucking turned on me. They joined the Legion and tried to kill me.

Kylie: Beth, we all tried to tell you to not go off with these thugs.

Beth: I've known them ever since I was in diapers. They were my family. They were even cool to you and the rest of the guys. How could I have known that they were turn on me?!

Beth makes a sharp turn past the remains of their old high school; Kylie nearly flies off of the motorcycle. Kylie's heart is racing as fast as Beth racing to where they need to go.

Kylie: BETH! Slow down! I nearly flew off the motorcycle.

Beth is so frustrated, she can't even hear Kylie as Kylie can hear Beth go off about the Road-Vipers. Kylie tries to get Beth's attention, but can't even hear herself think. This makes her furious as well.

Kylie (max-volume): BETH!!!

Beth makes a sudden stop at a four-way stop as if the traffic lights were not destroyed. This sudden stop sends Kylie flying off the

---

[22] Thunderbolt field-operative. Mystic-Cosmic EC hybrid. Wronged Safe-Guardian. Caucasian. Black hair. Black eyes. Shoulder Length Hair. American. Age 19.

[23] A gauntlet used by Safe-Guardians to allow a team to communicate with each other telepathically.

motorcycle; she bounces face first off of the pavement and then slides a yard from impact. While the suit is already damaged, Kylie took no damage from the impact; her shields did not even take damage. Beth dissipates the Tele-Link as she puts her hands over her ears, close to a headache.

Beth: Goddamn…, are you trying to blow my head off?!

Kylie slowly gets up while groaning. She slams her fist onto the street out being upset with Beth. Beth slowly rides up to Kylie to see if she's okay.

Beth: You alright, Kylie?

Kylie kicks Beth's motorcycle, sending it and Beth flying to a nearly cable tower. The force being put on the weakened tower causes it to timber away from them.

Beth: Kylie, what the fuck is wrong with you?
Kylie: Beth, just shut up and get over here!
Beth: Alright, geez.

Beth rides next to Kylie; Kylie gets on and they ride off back on the road. They ride at a normal speed through their hometown of Sterling Hills and drives in front of Kendall's house. Beth gets off of the bike and Kylie falls down the road out of exhaustion. She is breathing heavily as Beth's motorcycle dissipates.

Beth: Okay… maybe I was going a tad too fast and I was a tad angry and…
Kylie (irritated): Beth, don't talk to me right now.
Beth: How many more times do I have to say "Sorry?"
Kylie: Just stop talking and calm down.
Beth: Kylie, you have no idea what I'm going through.
Kylie: I know that you've tried to make good people out of psychopaths. We all told you that they could not be trusted. We told you about

all things they've said about you and even how they will kill you one day. But, you didn't listen to us. I told you this, Kendall told you this, Zack[24] told you this, Sheila[25], Christina[26], and Dom[27] told you the same thing…

Beth: Alright, alright, alright… I get it. I just didn't think that they would turn on me. I thought I was able to change. Okay, I made a mistake. Are you happy now?

Kylie: I'm just glad to know that you survived all of this chaos.

Kylie looks at the sky to see it is blocked out as the Earth is plunging into Nuclear Winter in the span of a week. Kylie can tell how much destruction has occurred as she can compare the Earth before the war and now. Kylie goes silent as she grows worried about her friends; Beth can see that Kylie is silent.

Beth: Are you okay, Kylie?

Kylie: I'm fine. Let's just go to the backyard.

Kylie and Beth go through Kendall's destroyed childhood home. Kylie and Beth grew up with Kendall, Zackery Batto, Dominic Stevens, Sheila Warrens, and Christina Sonic. As they go through the house, they begin to reminisce the countless adventures and misadventures they had as they all got older.

Beth: I really do wish things can go back to how they used to be. Back when we were all kids and didn't have a care in the world.

---

[24] Thunderbolt Field Operative and Weapon Specialist. Trained in the ways of the EC weaponry. Raised in a family of military men. Caucasian. Black Hair. Blue eyes. Curly Hair. Small scar on face. American. Age 20.

[25] Thunderbolt Field Operative. Runaway princess. Latina. Black Hair. Black eyes. Dark Brown skin. Long hair. Tribal marks on body. African. Age 20.

[26] Member of the small group of friends. Trained to fight by Kylie and housemate of Kendall. Has the most beautiful voice in Aurora, Colorado. Caucasian. Brunette. Brown eyes. long hair with barrettes. American. Age 19.

[27] Thunderbolt field operative. Duplicator-Deity. Caucasian. Blonde hair. Blue eyes. American. Age 19.

Kylie: Good times have to die, Beth.

Beth: Only if you let them die. If you play your cards right, then good times will be eternal.

Kylie: I only wish I can believe that.

They step into the backyard; Beth stands on the stairway and leans on the house as Kylie steps on the grass. She focuses E.C. energy in her hand and extends it. She can feel a wood wall in the palm of her hand and when she feels this, she fires a pulse from that hand and their childhood clubhouse appears after she makes it drop the magical invisibility and intangibility.

Beth: I have always thought that was cool.

Kylie (upset): Yeah... right.

Beth: What happened to that giant blue star that was on your face?

Kylie: You know I don't want to talk about?

Beth: What about Kyzo?

Kylie (irritated): Beth, please don't mention that bastard?

Beth: What's the big deal? I thought Kyzo was the new one you've feel in love with after you fell out of love Kendall. What happened with you two?

Kylie: <Sigh> If you really want to know, Kyzo took everything from me.

Beth: What do you mean?

Kylie: All the things I've done. All the pain an suffering I had to endure. It was all for nothing now. He ruined everything!

Beth: What did he do?

Beth can see Kylie is starting to cry; she tries to get close to put her hand on her shoulder to comfort her.

Kylie (rage): HE FRAMED ME FOR MURDER!!!

Beth (confused): What?

Kylie: Kyzo murdered an innocent, framed me for murder, and Safe-Guardian council of elders all believed him. They locked my Mystic Energy and they sent me back to the Cosmic Realm where I found Kendall in the Onyx. I swear I'm innocent, Beth!

Beth: Now I'm tell you to calm down. Look, I know you'd never kill an innocent person.

Beth begins to wonder if all of their friends are still alive.

Beth: Hey don't you still have your Magedallion[28] to see if everyone is still alive?

Kylie: No, Kyzo stole it when the Safe-Guards arrested me. I told them, but they didn't listen. Now I can't tell if anything happened to our friends, especially that knucklehead Kendall. He knocked me out before going to fight Kenneth on his own.

Beth: Even though his Energy Core is unstable?

Kylie: Exactly... Now I can't sense his energy anymore. I'm trying not to fear the worse.

Beth: Let's not worry about that right now. Right now, let's worry about getting what you need to get out of here first.

Kylie: <Sob> Right.

Beth opens the door into their old clubhouse to see that the interior is still intact. Beth begins to think of how she and the others used to spend most of their time in this place. She looks at the Flat-Screen, the couches, the game systems, the shooting range, tennis table, a dojo, and study area for school. Beth notices that some of the keepsakes they placed inside, Kendall's Ocarina and Christina's Hand-me-down Guitar, are missing. Beth snaps out of it when Kylie walks past her and opens a secret glove compartment and pulls out her special Elemental-Sword[29] that she had in the clubhouse case of emergencies. When she grabs the handle, she can feel the power rushing inside of her. She feels

---

[28] An item that Kylie gave to her best friends meant to keep them close to her. If opened, the Magedallion will shine seven lights for herself and her six closet friends: Red for Kylie Shulls, Orange for Dominic Thomas, Yellow for Zackery Batto, Green for Sheila Warrens, Blue for Kendall Knighten Jr., Indigo for Christina Sonic, and Violet for Bethlehem Khat.

[29] An Enchanted Sword that allows the user to wield all of the elements: Fire, Ice, Water, Terra, Lightning, and Wind. Kylie crafted it before she became a full member of the Safe-Guardian order.

like she has her magic again as she holds it in air. She then looks at Beth; Beth looks impressed and she conjures he E.C. Pistols and holds them in a crossing barrels. Kylie places the tip of her Elemental Sword on the barrels of Beth's guns. Both feel powerful as they did back when they were all kids together; they felt unstoppable.

Beth: I think it's time we get the payback we're both due. Starting with the Road-Vipers.
Kylie: Yeah. Let's go.

Kylie and Beth dissipate their weapons as they leave the clubhouse, making it reactivate it's magic invisibility and intangibility. They quickly cut through the house and go back to the driveway. Beth conjures her E.C. Motorcycle fully started; they get on with Beth driving and Kylie in the back. Kylie holds on to Beth and Beth dashes out of the driveway. They ride back to Denver with their morale high and minds calmed, ready to strike down those who have wrong them.

CHAPTER IV
Fool's Errand

With the Legion spread across the entire planet, numerous enemies of their reign are either dead, imprisoned, or struggling to survive. With their advanced technology created by the Ultranian empire, the Legion is able to locate their enemies with ease and eliminate any form of rebellion in the past week of their control of the entire planet. To the eyes of the civilians who survived, the lucky ones are the ones who died fighting and living to fight another day is suicide. The hope of defeating the Legion is looked at as nothing more than a suicidal fool's errand. But, there are still those who are both brave and foolish enough to continue this fight to preserve the freedom of Earth and Humanity.

There is only few prisoners inside of the Mundi Castle Dungeon that are worthy of being held as prisoners instead of trophies. The Mundi Castle Dungeon is as old as the castle itself. The cells are ancient, dark, dank, rat infested, and have been deprived of hope for centuries. These cells held some of the most powerful beings that the Earth has ever known and now it holds inmates and warriors so dangerous and so psychotic, even the Legion cannot control them. These inmates are tied up so they cannot move, blind-folded so they cannot see, ears plugged so they cannot hear, and are gagged so they cannot talk; their noses are open so they can breathe. Inside of one of the cells is Peter Orion[30], who is neither gagged, nor plugged ears, nor blind-folded, and is wearing the same type of torn-up, dirty, stained, prisoner uniform that Tom and Jamie is wearing. He sits in the cell in despair, his spirit cracked, and in

---

[30] Thunderbolt weapon's specialist. First Lieutenant to Tom Sullivan. Human containing Ultranian DNA. African-American. Black hair. Short hair. Brown eyes. American. Age 20.

a state of lamenting as he reminisces the memories he had with someone who he loved, memories of the past before this war started. As he looks back at these memories, he feels sadness and a massive amount of anger for everything that has happened ever since the Legion first attacked two years ago. A stream of tears falls down Peter's face as he is looking at the bracelet that was given to him by the love of his life.

Peter (despair): Isabel... I'm so sorry. I... I couldn't save you. <Sob> Please forgive me.
Dungeon-Master: Come on, bro. I thought that you were a tough nigger. Tough niggers don't cry.

Peter rapidly gets back on his feet when he sees the Dungeon-Master, alongside the Warden with the new prisoners: Tom Sullivan and Jamie Kelly. He sees that Tom is on the Warden's shoulder and Jamie being held and touched by the Dungeon-Master.

Peter (shocked): What the fuck?! Captain?! Jamie?!
The Warden: Are you certain that these cells will hold these Thunderbolts, Dungeon-Master?
Dungeon-Master (confident): These cells have been built to hold beings that are far more powerful than these Thunderbolt kids. I'm positive they can hold. They can probably even hold Dark-Knighten and his strongest elites.
The Warden (annoyed): Thousands of years ago. The cells might've aged.
Dungeon-Master (persistent): They'll hold. They're still hold those loose cannons in the other cells as we speak. These can most certainly hold these little punks.
The Warden: I hope so. For your sake.

The Dungeon-Master opens the cell right across from Peter's cell; he and the Warden throws Tom and Jamie into the cell; Tom get thrown first and Jamie lands on Tom. The Warden, under the orders of Dark-Knighten, takes out a Healing-Orb[31], activates it, and drops it inside the cell, healing the wounds that Tom and Jamie sustained from Dark-Knighten's shotgun blasts and the beatings from the Legion soldiers. The healing continues as until both are healed; Tom's black eye is gone and his tooth is healed. Drained of energy, Jamie regains consciousness inside the cell. Jamie gets on her knees as she sits up off of Tom, who is still unconscious.

Jamie (drained): Where are we?
Dungeon-Master: In hell, sugar tits.

The Dungeon-Master leaves the dungeon in order to escort the Warden out of the castle.

Jamie: Captain, wake up! Come on Captain, wake up!
Tom: Ugh…, Jamie?
Jamie: <Sigh of relief> It's me, Captain. You have to get up.
Tom: What happened? Where are we?
Peter (depressed): We're inside the dungeon of the castle.

Tom and Jamie direct their attention to where the voice came from and they see Peter in the cell across from them. Jamie is happy to see that Peter is still alive; Tom is too riddled with.

Jamie (ecstatic): Oh my God, Peter, is that you?
Peter (depressed): Yeah Jamie… it's me. At least you two are still alive.
Tom: Peter, what happened to you? We lost contact with you and Isabel about four days ago.
Jamie: Yeah, and where is Isabel? She left with you to that destress call mission.

---

[31] An Ultranian grenade, used by both Onyx and Legion, that can heal any and all physical wounds. Records show of these grenade even being able to heal and regenerate amputated limbs through biotic healing technology.

Peter looks away from them and begins to let tears fall from his face, wondering how to tell them. From the look on Peter's face, Tom can tell what he is about to tell them.

Peter (lamenting): Captain... Jamie... I-I'm sorry. Isabel... Isabel didn't make it.

Jamie, trying to contemplate the news of her best friend, turns and then leans to the wall with tears. Tom's body wants to collapse on the knees, but he knows that he has to stay strong.

Tom: What happened to her?

As Peter explains what happened, anger inside begins to seep out into the open.

Peter: We were sent on a mission four days ago. Isabel and I were sent to locate the source of an emergency transmission from a command post that was under attack by the Legion. But, it was a trap. We were ambushed by Omegatronus. He shot me with an EMP charge, short circuit my Mark I's[32] systems. We didn't stand a chance against him. He overpowered us both even with Isabel's biotic tech on hand. He was going to deliver the final blow by ramming his blade in my chest and... Isabel... Isabel jumped in the way. It instantly killed her. I tried to tear him apart, but my suit was too low on power and took too much damage to do anything. Then... he fired some powerful weapon he has and a single shot from it completely destroyed the Mark I. I nearly died there and then, but I didn't. I survived long enough to wish I didn't. And when I woke up, I was

---

[32] The Advance One-of-a-kind battle suit that Peter created for himself. Equipped with weapon converter systems to convert the armor on his arms into high-powered Ultranian weapons, blueprints to powerful Ultranian weapons, armored plating made from Ultranian medal strong enough to withstand Ultranian repulser fire, propulsion systems to allow him to fly, rechargeable shields, compatibility to his personal Ultranian jet called The Omega-Star, a highly advanced A.I. named "Apex", and an environmental that allows his suit to change for certain environments.

here in this cell with that robotic bastard on the other side. He killed her and I couldn't save her.

Tom can see that Peter's spirit is broken as he can see Peter's Self-Pity after losing the one he truly loved.

Tom: It wasn't your fault, Peter.

Peter (deep sadness): How was it not my fault? She sacrificed herself to save me, captain! I wasn't strong enough. My suit wasn't strong enough. She's dead because of me. Now we're going to die next. Hell, we can be the last Thunderbolts for all I know.

Jamie: Peter, stop beating yourself up. It's not over, yet.

Peter: <Chuckles> Right, is this the part where you say Isabel would not want to see me like this? We'll never know that now because she's dead. She died right in front of me, Jamie. Sorry if I can't help, but beat myself up.

Jamie (desperate): Peter's gone demented. Captain, we need to get out of here.

Tom: Jamie, calm down!

Jamie: Captain, Kendall is dead. Isabel is dead. And if we do not get out of here, we will be next. We need to get out of here, Captain!

Tom: I can't even hear myself think!

Peter (depressed): What's the point of trying to escape? We can't win this fight. We're all going to die. We'll just delay the inevitable even if we manage to escape.

Jamie: Peter… you're just going to give up.

Peter: They're way too strong for us. We've got into a fight that we can't possibly win. We've lost.

Jamie cannot believe that she is hearing Peter, someone who has never given up in the past, is beginning to give up. She takes out her torn-up, rigid shoe off her right foot and throws it at Peter's head, right in the nose. The impact of the shoes caused a massive amount of pain.

Peter (agony): Augh… shit! Motherfuck! What the fuck, Jamie?

Jamie (irritated): That was to knock some sense into your thick skull. How can you possibly give up, Peter? You would never give up in the past and yes, Isabel would never let you give up on something you're passionate about. Why the hell are you giving up now? We have to keep fighting.

Peter (irritated): How the fuck can we possibly fight back now? Magnus is destroyed, the entire Onyx army is spread thin across Earth, we don't know if other Thunderbolts are still alive, and we're here in the castle from hell waiting to die. How can we keep fighting?

Jamie: We've always found a way before. We can find a way now. We're not going to do it by putting our heads in the sand and sticking out our asses to just take whatever they throw at us.

Peter: We may not have a choice if we want to stay breathing. We can't find a way this time. They've gotten too powerful. We're hopelessly outnumbered and outgunned. Even if we do manage to find a way out of here, The Legion will just find and kill us on the spot. They're getting stronger and stronger and we can't stop them! <Sigh> Let's face facts Jamie, we're completely, utterly fucked.

A light begins to beep on Tom's wrist and an Ultranian tracker bracelet appears as it's invisibility and intangibility modes deactivate.

Apex: Voice confirmed. Ready to commence Mark II Protocol.

Peter and Jamie turn their attention to Tom after hearing Apex's voice.

Peter: Apex?

A memory instantly comes into Tom's head about where he got that bracelet and at moment, he instantly comes up with a plan. Tom quickly takes it off his wrist and looks at Peter.

Tom: Peter, catch!
Tom throws the bracelet at Peter; Peter catches it.

Peter: Why are you two just throwing stuff at me like I'm a zoo animal.

Jamie (quietly, urgently): <Shush> Somebody's coming.

The Dungeon-Master opens the door to the dungeons after returning from the "enlightening" conversation with the Warden. As he returns, he hears the commotion. He has his Ultranian shotgun out to intimidate the prisoner, despite only the imprisoned Thunderbolts can see and hear him.

Dungeon-Master: Hey! What's going on over here?

Before the they get into the Dungeon-master's sight, Tom taps his left wrist to let Peter know to put the bracelet on his wrist; Peter puts the bracelet on his left wrist with his hands behind his back and it reactivate its invisibility and intangibility modes.

Jamie (innocent impression): We're not doing anything.

Peter: Yeah, we're just adjusting to the last moments in this <cringe> lovely dungeon. <Fake cough> Shitsty.

Dungeon-Master: That's funny... Because I heard someone say something about throwing stuff. He sees Jamie's shoe in Peter's cell floor.

Dungeon-Master: Then what's that?

Jamie: Oh, that's my shoe. You see, Peter over there said something stupid and I had to throw my shoe at his face to knock some sense into him. Peter couldn't catch a beachball falling in slow-motion.

Peter: That shoe hurt like a bitch too.

The Dungeon-Master looks at the shoe print bruise on Peter's face and then looks at Jamie's face sincere face. He thinks of what to do and then he suddenly laughs out loud.

Dungeon-Master (amused): That's funny. I like you even more now, Monkey-Girl. You're going to have a good time with me on guard.

The Dungeon-Master has his hand next on his belt with his fingertips near his crotch. Jamie hides her cringe in her fake face.

Jamie (disgusted): I bet I am.

Jamie waits until he leaves the Dungeon.

Jamie (mad): Ugly-ass pervert! We need to kill that Quasimodo-looking mother...

Peter: Jamie... do you want him to come back and shot our asses? Keep it down. Captain, why do you have an Ultranian tracker on you?

Tom: Never mind that. Just activate the Mark II protocol.

Jamie: "Mark II protocol?"

Peter thinks about what the Mark II protocol is and remembers it full and well.

Peter: "Mark II?" How do you know about the Mark II?

Jamie: What are you talking about? What's "the Mark II?"

Peter: It's a new battle suit that I've designed to be more powerful than the Mark I. But, it's defective. I tried to use it numerous times and it failed every single time. I modified several times and nothing worked. So, I scrapped the idea of a new Battle-Suit.

Tom: Apex said he secretly modified it every single time you modified the Mark I, making it far stronger than the Mark I. He said it shouldn't be defective anymore.

Peter: Captain, how do you know that?

Tom (annoyed): Peter, you're asking too many questions. Just say "Initiate Mark II Protocol" into the bracelet. That's an order.

Peter: Yes sir. Apex, initiate the Mark II protocol.

Apex: Mark II protocol initiated. Initiating final preparations. Estimated Time: Twenty-Four hours.

Peter: Okay. Now what?

Jamie: Is this part of a plan, Captain?

Tom: Yes, we're getting out of here and we are going to make Dark-Knighten pay for what he's done.

Peter (doubtful): Okay Captain, how are we going to escape? The Mark II isn't even finished yet.

Tom (to Peter): It's simple… We're going to wait for you are going to get the Mark II to bust us out. And if I'm right, it should be here just in time for your execution.

Peter: Wait… WHAT?!

Jamie: Execution?

Tom sighs with all of the questions and decides it is his turn to ask questions. He gets up, tears a piece of his pants sleeves around his ankles off, takes off his extremely uncomfortable shoes, and walks next to the cell bars.

Tom (shouting): EXCUSE ME, MR. DUNGEON-MASTER! HEY!!!

Tom gets no response and decides to take drastic measures. He tears up the pieces of clothes to give to Jamie next to him. He throws a couple pieces to Peter.

Tom: Use that to plug your ears.

Jamie: Captain, what are you?

Tom plugs his ears with the pieces he has and starts banging on the cell bars with his shoes in order to attract the Dungeon-Master. The cell bars are designed to create high frequency whenever a prisoner would try to break down the cells. The frequencies would cause the prisoner to cease their resistance. Tom plugging his ears would stop the frequencies from entering his ears as he prepares to do something highly uncharacteristic.

Tom (shouting): HEY, WE NEED TO SEE YOUR UGLY-ASS FACE!!! I HAVE A QUESTION THAT ONLY YOU CAN ANSWER! IT'S ABOUT WHEN WE'LL DIE! GET IN HERE!!!

The noise is so loud, Jamie and Peter cover their ears out of reflex. They both quickly cover and plug their ears with the pieces of clothing, but it only cuts the volume in half. Jamie, being in the same cell as Tom, gets on her hands and knees with her tail around her head to cover her ears, feeling like her ears were beginning to bleed. To Peter, the banging is louder than the sound of a kitchen knife on a chalkboard; he heard that sound before. Tom stops when he hears the chamber doors stop.

Peter: Goddamn, what the fuck are those shoes made of?

The Dungeon-Master quickly walks in front of Tom and Jamie's cell.

Dungeon-Master (irritated): The hell's going on over here?!
Tom: Care to remind Peter here what happens in the next twenty-four hours?

The Dungeon-Master humorously chuckles while turning to Peter, puts his arm over his head, and pulls his arm up, implementing a lynching because Peter is African-American.

Peter: Okay, what the actual fuck?
Dungeon-Master (to Tom): Twenty-Four from now and we will have one less monkey in this world and I'm not talking about her. Does that answer your question, inmate?
Tom: It's a start.
Dungeon-Master: Good... Now stop banging on the damn cell! They don't pay me enough of this shit.

Dungeon-Master walks out of the dungeon again.

Peter: Captain, I agree with Jamie. We need to kill that motherfucker before we leave here.
Tom: You'll get your chance. We'll have to go through him in order bust us out. Right now, we'll just have to wait here.
Jamie: In this dank, rat infested dungeon for twenty-four hours, Captain? We're just going to wait hear while everyone else is out

there fighting and dying out there? There's not even a toilet in here. How do we use the bathroom here?

Peter: Uh, Jamie... Why do you think this place smells like dead bodies, piss, and shit?

Jamie gets close to throw up as she can see the dried up excrement in the corner of her cell. Tom looks at Jamie with a smirk on his face.

Tom: Jamie, do you have any other place to wait? Do you have a way to contact everyone else? No... Thought so. Now then, getting captured by Foreman in an ambush, getting beaten as a P.O.W., getting shot, and getting put in a filthy prison made me tired. I'm going to take a nap.

Peter: We're just going to sit here and I have to wait to die? Come on, Captain.

Tom: Calm down, Peter. We need to wait for the right moment to strike. Now is not that time.

Tom goes to sleep on the old, floppy bed. Peter and Jamie did not expect to see Tom wait so patiently. They were expecting an instant escape plan, not to wait in the cell for twenty-four hours.

Peter: Jamie, can you believe this? We have to wait here in this shitsty.

Jamie: At least we have a plan now. Have faith in the Captain, Peter. He never fail us before, he won't fail us now. We'll make that tin-can Omegatronus get what he deserves. Right now, let's just wait for the right time like the Captain said.

Jamie leans back on the wall and sits down on her butt on the ground.

Peter falls on his bed with his arms on his knees.

Peter (to himself): Yeah, we really are fucked now. Having to relay on a defective suit to fight against the biggest stronghold in the universe.

Everyone decide to wait in the dungeon with no fuss and no more commotion. When one hour no commotion passes, the Dungeon-Master suspects that they are up to something. As a result, he decides to call Gordon in order to increase security in the dungeons in case if they are to attempt to escape.

Chapter V
The Grand Escape

As the twenty-four hours pass, the Thunderbolts begin to rebuild their strength in order for their plan to commence and succeed. Tom is looking around as he thinks of the strategy, Jamie is sitting on the ground playing with her hard as rock food to pass the time, and Peter is laying down counting the cracks in the ceiling, reaching 3,746. While counting the cracks in the ceiling, Peter thinks about the way things used to be for the Thunderbolts, back when he, Tom, Jamie, Isabel Stratton[33], Jacob Stevens[34], Bridgette, and Anthony "Tony" Vane[35] were just simply an elite Onyx strike-team, Omega-Squad[36]. Peter reminisces the good times that they had from the day they all met, their very first mission together, when he and Isabel fell in love, living in the large metropolis that used to be Magnus, and how it all changed when Agent-Thomas[37] and Kendall joined Omega and it became the

---

[33] Thunderbolt Medical Officer. The Onyx Valkyrie. Peter's friend turned lover. Jamie's best female friend. Caucasian. Blonde hair. Blue eyes. Long hair. K.I.A. Swiss. Age 20

[34] Thunderbolt Field-operative/ Interrogator. The bane of all secrets. Tom's rival in fighting skill. Caucasian. Black hair. Black eyes. Curly hair. M.I.A. Age 19

[35] Thunderbolt Mechanical officer. The most highly skilled builder in the entire Onyx army. In a romantic relationship with Jacob. Hispanic. Blonde hair. Green eyes. M.I.A. age 18.5

[36] The most elite strike Team of the entire Onyx army. Made of the best soldiers that the Onyx can assemble. Operated like a family. Taking on missions that others wouldn't even dream of and accomplish every single mission.

[37] Thunderbolt Elite Field-officer. Trained by the former Generalissimo of the Thunderbolts. Known for not adjusting to following order from those other than the one who trained him. M.I.A. Age 19.

Thunderbolts-Division. Remembering all of the good old day is causing more tears to fall from Peter's eyes.

While she is playing with her food to keep herself amused and scratching her back with her tail, Jamie remembers how she used to be part of the Shin International Circus and how she spent her young childhood being the star attraction of the show that everyone wanted to see, the Monkey-Girl. But, little did everyone know back then, Jamie was shunned, neglected, and abused by the other performers and under unfortunate circumstances, she was found by Richard Sullivan and a young Tom Sullivan when she was nine. She remembers how Tom was her very first friend because Tom did not seeing her as a circus freak, but as a friend. The only one who did not see her as a freak before was her teacher, Barton. He trained and raised her to embrace her existence as a Deity[38] as he was a former member of the B.O.G[39] and made her an honorary member of the Brotherhood. He gives her the B.O.G symbol tattoo on her left arm as a symbol of her embracing her gifts and he gave her the nickname, "Wukong". Looking at the tattoo, she remembers how she met Jack Turbo[40] and how they grew close as the war escalated, leading her to worry about him and hoping that he is still alive. She grabs the B.O.G symbol tattoo as she thinks about how could actually die and never see Jack again and possibly be Barton where she thinks he went.

Tom thinks about when he obtained his motivation to continue fighting, to never give up, and to fight until his dying breath. When he was seven in his academy days, during his excruciating hand-to-hand combat training using a brass knuckles and a manikin with Richard. In this training, he learned how to use a brass-knuckle and where to hit in order to bring an enemy down quickly. Richard noticed that Tom began

---

[38] A human who possesses super powers. 50% of all humans on Earth possess powers. Possess a long history of slavery, suffering, and prejudice that all Deities know about.

[39] Brotherhood of Gods

[40] Thunderbolt field-operative. Former member of the B.O.G. Oldest of the Turbo siblings. Fire-Deity. A man who was destined to loss. Caucasian. Black hair. Inferno Red eye. Wears an Eyepatch over his Lightning White left eye. Straight hair. Age 23.

to wan in performance out of exhaustion and lack of determination and he stated that soldiers never give up. This lead young Tom to ask Richard, "Commander, why do soldiers never give up?" and Richard answered, "Because soldiers are the only ones who must fight for those who cannot fight for themselves. They have to fight with all they have. Innocents will die if they don't." "But, what if things get so hard for the soldiers, they can't continue to fight?" "Tom, let me tell a quote that will always inspires me to continue to keep fighting, even when it seems too hard to keep fighting. This is a quote from Winston Churchill…, now I want you to listen to this quote carefully because this is my motivation and hopefully yours in the future. He said, 'If you're going through hell, keep going.' This means never give up and stay strong. Remember these words, Tom, you may need them in the future" "Yes sir." "Alright, let's get back to training." Tom held on to these words ever since then and he vowed to never give up and to always stay strong no matter what type of hell he would go through. This memory causes Tom to shed a tear.

Peter: Hey Jamie, do you remember when things for us were a lot simpler?

Jamie: I can remember being a circus performer. Back when people called me "Monkey-Girl." That was simple.

Peter: Captain, what was simple for you?

Tom: Holding up after the Enhancement Program was surprising simple.

Peter: How about how we used to take on mobsters, mad scientists, and monsters? Back when things were easy instead of the Ultranian empire, ancient villains, people with a power dangerous enough to destroy the Universe, and people who had been revived from the dead just to fight and beat *us*… I actually miss the old days, back when we were all together and there weren't that many of us to worry about.

Jamie: I know how you feel, Peter. I miss the days of Omega-Squad too. Back when missions were adventures and not war stories. But, reminiscing the glory days won't bring them back. We have to keep fighting as we don't become a memory as well.

Peter: At this point, we may very be a memory. I'm telling you, we're
  in over our...
Jamie (irritated): Do you want me to throw my shoe at you again?
  Because I will.
Peter: You wouldn't dare.

Jamie takes off her shoe with her tail and pretends to fling it,
making Peter flinch with his eyes shut and his hands in front of his face
to brace for impact. When he notices that nothing hit his face this time,
he looks at Jamie to see the smirk on her face; she made him flinch.

Jamie (amused): Flinch.
Peter: Jamie, you can be a bully, you know that? The type of bully who
  doesn't get their ass whooped, too.
Jamie: Yeah... because I care, Peter.
Peter (amused): <Laughs> Fucking asshole.

The Dungeon-Master walks back inside of the dungeon. Jamie
realizes that twenty-four hours have passed.

Jamie (urgency): Captain...

Tom looks at the Dungeon-Master, the armed guards protecting
him, and the executioner. He realizes that the time to strike is here. Peter
is not even looking at the Dungeon-Master and who the executioner is.

Peter: It's about time you showed up, I'm ready to be out this old
  dungeon. I thought Antonio's room was a real...
Omegatronus: Hello, Orion. You appear well.

Peter rapidly gets on his feet in a bid of rage, wanting to tear the
executioner, Omegatronus, apart. He bangs on the cell bars as he is
consumed with rage for the one who killed Isabel.

Peter: You son of a bitch!!!

Omegatronus grabs Peter by the shirt and pulls him into the cell bars with enough force to have him bounce from the cell bars and back onto the ground.

Omegatronus: I am afraid that our little feud ends today. Open the cell!

The Dungeon-Master opens the cell; Peter gets up and, without even thinking, punches Omegatronus in the face with all of his might. The punch does not phase Omegatronus in the slightest, in fact Peter nearly breaks his knuckles. Omegatronus grabs Peter by the neck, lifts him up in the air, and throws him at the wall. Peter can barely stand after this, but he does not care about the pain; the one thing he cares about was seeing Omegatronus die. Omegatronus softly jabs Peter in the stomach before he gets a chance to try another futile and annoying attack; Peter coughs up spit and gets on his knees. Peter cannot get up off his knees after taking major damage.

Omegatronus: I see that you still have some fight left in you. But, we'll see if you can fight your way out of the grave.

Jamie grows angry as she watches Peter getting beaten, but she knows she cannot do anything about it. Meanwhile, Tom leans back on the wall calmly doing nothing.

Tom: Calm down, Jamie.
Jamie: Captain, he's beating Peter. We can't just sit here and do nothing.
Tom: We aren't doing nothing. We're being patient.

Omegatronus puts Ultranian handcuffs on Peter to lock his hands, lifts Peter on his feet, and takes him outside the cell. Omegatronus converts his arm into the Ultranian assault rifle and puts the barrel in Peter's back. Peter stands still knowing that one Ultranian repulser blast can kill a human and beings with far stronger biology with just a single blast. Instead of retaliating, he uses his neural connection with Apex to initiate the Mark II protocol.

Omegatronus: Continue to fight and you will die sooner.

Peter: Why don't you kill me now? Why didn't you kill me when you have every opportunity right in front of you?

Omegatronus: Because the Dark-Knighten wants to make an example out of all Thunderbolts; that includes you. Now move it!

Omegatronus pushes Peter forward in order for him to walk. In a split second, Peter looks at Tom and Tom smirks at Peter while Peter is still nervous. Omegatronus, with no suspicion, takes Peter outside of the cell and the Dungeon-Master looks at both Tom and Jamie.

Dungeon-Master (curious): Not even going to say goodbye to your friend?

Tom: Don't worry... We won't have to.

Dungeon-Master: What is that supposed to mean?

Tom: We'll see him again... One way or another.

The Dungeon-Master looks at Tom with a grin on his face and then walks away.

Jamie (worried): Captain, how do we know if this plan will work?

Tom (calmly): We don't. It's on Peter now. I have confidence in him.

Jamie wants to put her faith in Tom like she has in the past without hesitation, but she is too concerned and has too much uncertainty in her to immediately put her faith in Tom the way she used to.

Jamie (worried): I hope this plan of yours works, Captain. It's all we've got.

Tom: I know.

A few minutes of walking have passed. Omegatronus, accompanied by Legion guards, is escorting Peter to the sight of his execution: The

Mundi Inferno-Pit[41]. There are hundreds of Legion soldiers both guarding and spectating the execution in the towers around the pit. The soldiers are armed with heavy Ultranian firearms and hand-to-hand combat tools in case there would be any interruptions to the execution. They cheer and go wild like they are watching their home country win the FIFA World Cup. Peter stops to wonder why there are so many people in an execution, but he did not have time to think about it as Omegatronus pushes forward. As he walks to the pit, Peter begins to have a mild tingling feeling in his head. Apex contacts Peter through the Neural-Link Peter installed two weeks ago.

Apex: Peter, can you hear me?

Peter (telepathically): Apex, is that you?

Apex: Affirmative.

Peter: How can you be talking to me right now?

Apex: Through the Neural-Link you installed two weeks ago.

Peter: Oh… I don't know how I forgot that.

Apex: The Mark II is inbound to your location, all you have to do is call for it and it will come to you.

Peter: Apex, I don't know if you can see it, but I am surrounded and Omegatronus destroyed the Mark I.

Apex: The Mark II can help you escape as Dark-Knighten is not located in the castle or anywhere on Earth.

Peter: What do you mean he's not on Earth?

Apex: Dark-Knighten possesses a large energy signal due to his immense power. His signal faded away. Without him, the Mark II can most certainly help you escape.

Peter: Alright, this suit better not still be defective or I'm fucked.

Omegatronus stops Peter by grabbing his shirt, waiting for the time to go onto the leap ledge.

---

[41] The Pit full of molten lava in Mundi village. Located in the rear of the castle, the pit acts as the entrance to the pits of Hell, where the guilty will plunge into damnation.

Omegatronus: You have always been, as you humans say, a thorn in my side. I have had numerous foes from numerous parts of the Universe, but you would constantly interfere in my affairs. You would even stain the trust I have earned in my former master by getting in my way. But now, I no longer have share this existence with you. Do you have any last words, Orion?

Peter: Yeah… I'm not going to die. Can't say the same for you.

Omegatronus: Poor choice of words.

Omegatronus takes Peter to the end of the leap ledge, both are surrounded by the boos aimed for Peter. Peter looks at the crowd and he sees that there are cameras in every corner of the towers, broadcasting to every single Legion-City all over the world as everyone wants to see the notorious Peter Orion get executed. In the Inferno-Pit, a Legion General walks out of the castle behind Peter and Omegatronus and he stops behind them with a microphone connected to a speakers all over the Inferno-Pit. He talks through the cheers and boos.

Legion General: My fellow Legion brothers and sisters, we are here today for the execution of Peter Orion. As you all know, Peter Orion is one of the most dangerous Thunderbolts. This particular Thunderbolt has caused the deaths of countless Legion brothers and sister and has gotten in the way of the formation of the new world. And now, he is here to receive justice for standing in the way of the reformation of the planet! Peter Orion, have you any last words before you make your way into hell?

Peter (To Apex, Telepathically): Set the timer for five seconds.

Peter gets on the microphone as the microphone is near us.

Peter: Um… two things actually. One, what you call "justice," I like to call "A pile of steaming hot horse-shit." And two for the cameras, the real show has just started.

Peter looks up and hears the sound of the Omega-Star[42] soaring through the skies, controlled by Apex via Auto-Pilot. The Omega-Star flies over the pit and it drops an EMP bomb. The soldiers, with Ultranian battle armor that is venerable to EMPs, scatter across the pit, trying to evade the blast. But, the EMP bomb detonates on the air low enough for the blast radius to spread through the entire pit. This blast temporarily jams the systems of everyone in the entire pit, permanently disables the cameras, and throws Omegatronus off balance due; being a Battle-Android, Omegatronus is extremely venerable to Ultranian-Level EMPs. Peter, who isn't effected in the slightest, notices that Omegatronus's systems are jammed from the blast and hits Omegatronus in the head with his handcuffs. The impact mildly straightens Omegatronus's optics and Omegatronus kicks Peter off the ledge, but Peter put his cuff in the way of the kick, breaking the cuffs and freeing his hands, but is still falling towards the pit.

Peter: Apex, drop it now!

The Omega-Star drops the Mark II[43], controlled by the autopilot. The Mark II flies towards Peter and reaches him before he falls into the Inferno-Pit. When the suit reaches him, the autopilot quickly scans his wristband to authorize his identity and suits him up, armoring him from head-to-toe. Peter splashes into the pit when gains control of the suit. Omegatronus's systems steadies itself by the time Peter falls into the Inferno-Pit. When Omegatronus looks down at the pit to scan for Peter's life signal, he sees that Peter is in the pit. Omegatronus steels himself for whatever Peter is planning. He redirects his attention to the Omega-Star for a split-second.

[42] Peter's personal Ultranian fighter-jet. Containing homing missiles, gatling guns, a cloaking shield, a signal shielder, EMP shields, battlefield shields, a repair station (originally for the Mark I), a drop station, ETC.
[43] The formerly defective upgraded battle suit with greater power than the Mark I could ever be. Equipped with blueprints to more powerful weapons, 5x stronger and flexible armored plating, more efficient propulsion systems, an environment adaptor in order to adjust to any and every environment, more advanced scanners, shoulder sentry guns, and a compatibility link with the Omega-Star.

Omegatronus: Eliminate that ship!

He detects an anomaly in the pit and looks down to scan that pit to detect Peter's signal. Peter is standing in the bottom of the Inferno-Pit with his shields keeping him from being melted alive. Peter charges the energy in his hand to activate a shockwave powerful enough to send most the lava in the pit up in the air. He fires the shockwave and the amount of force the shockwave causes the lava in the pit to erupt resembling a volcano, catching Omegatronus off-guard. As the lava flies up in the air, Peter activates a barrier to trap the lava in the air and attract more lava from the pit to float around as he flies to the center of the plunge. To the soldiers and Omegatronus, it looks an orb of molten lava floating in the air that is compressing; they begin to open fire on the orb. Peter, inside the molten orb, sees that his shields are at 85% from the molten lava that is getting hotter from the energy of the barrier. He balls up and charges the barrier around him and thrust his arms and legs outward, expanding the barrier to send the lava flying into the soldiers, managing to melt through their Ultranian armor and melting half of them alive while the rest get gunned down by the Omega-Star. Omegatronus uses his shields to protect himself. He looks up to see Peter floating in the Mark II with its colors black and neon-blue, the colors of the Onyx.

Peter: You were right, Omegatronus. Only one of us will die here!

Omegatronus opens fire on Peter, but Peter does not stagger, even with the barrier being lowered to it's standard shielding. Peter charges repulser energy in his fist and slams down in front of Omegatronus, making him fly backwards with moderate damage. Peter thrusts into Omegatronus; Omegatronus recovers just in time, and the two collide their right fists, creating a powerful shockwave. Peter and Omegatronus both know that only one of them will walk away alive. Peter charges energy in his left fist and Omegatronus readies his left fist and they collide again, creating another powerful shockwave. Omegatronus kicks Peter and Peter rapidly recovers; he then steels himself for Omegatronus's next attack. Omegatronus fires his propulsers and thrusts at Peter to throw a large amount of high powered punches at Peter, who blocks his punches. Peter takes all of Omegatronus's punches which is only lowering the Mark II's rechargeable shields; eventually Peter manages to grab both of Omegatronus's arm in order to stop the punches. Peter holds on to his arms; Omegatronus cannot break free. He then knees him in the chin and kicks him back to the leap ledge. Peter then quickly converts his suit's right arm armor into an Ultranian rocket-launcher, capable of firing four rockets at once. He quickly target-locks Omegatronus and fires the four rockets. The rockets hit Omegatronus full force before he gets a chance to recover on the ledge. Omegatronus still stands with static around him showing that he has taken major damage. Peter lands in the ledge, converts his rocket launcher into a Ultranian Arm-Blade and dashes to Omegatronus. He deals massive damage to Omegatronus with two slashes from his sword. Omegatronus blocks a third slash with his left arm converted into an Ultranian Arm-Blade, converts his available arm into the Neutron-Cannon[44] and blasts Peter in the chest. The blast only sends Peter flying back with half of his shields depleted. Omegatronus fires another blast and Peter deflects the blast to the side with his sword. Omegatronus directs all of his reserve power to the Neutron-Cannon to give it rapid fire and fires numerous blasts at Peter; Peter deflects all of the blasts in numerous directions with his sword.

Apex: Peter, reinforcements are approaching. You don't have much time.
Peter (preoccupied): I know that! But, I'm not leaving until I turn him into scrap.

When Peter deflects the last blast, he sees Omegatronus in the air with his Ultranian Arm-Blade ready split his head; Peter holds his sword up to block it. They begin to clash swords with every intent to kill. Peter is running out of stamina, causing him to slow down, while Omegatronus has infinite stamina being non-organic. Omegatronus

---

[44] Omegatronus's most powerful firearm. The same weapon that destroyed the Mark I with one blast.

lands a punch on Peter's face and kicks him back and Peter fall on his rear. Omegatronus thrusts his sword forward to impale Peter's heart, but Peter's shoulder sentries open fire on him, dealing even more damage to Omegatronus, some even going through his armor. Omegatronus gets on one knee. Peter, with this gap of time, quickly gets up and ram his blade into Omegatronus's chest. The blade goes right through Omegatronus's power core. Omegatronus is rapidly losing power as his power core has been critically damaged. Peter directly into Omegatronus's eyes.

Peter: Any last words?
Omegatronus: You'll die by hands of the Legion, Orion.

Peter activate the cannon in his sword to blast a hole in Omegatronus, destroying his power core. The light emanating from Omegatronus's body goes out as he falls back; meaning he is dead. Peter, not satisfied, stomps on Omegatronus's head in to crush his processor to make sure he cannot come back.

Peter: I don't think so.

Peter deactivates his sentries, converts his right arm back to normal, and takes a deep breath knowing that he just avenged Isabel. His moral has been boosted to his normal amount, high.

Apex: I have taken the liberty of activating a Translocator-Cube with
    the Mark II's autopilot. You can translocate back to the Omega-Star
    when you find Captain Sullivan and Agent Kelly.
Peter: Apex, you're a genius. Fly the Omega-Star into the ocean and
    mark a path to the Captain and Jamie.

Apex highlights the path from the Inferno-Pit to Tom and Jamie's cell in the dungeon.

Apex: Path highlighted. Destination marked.
Peter: Good… Tom, Jamie, we are breaking out of this bitch.

Minutes pass after Peter defeated Omegatronus, numerous Legion guards in the castle mobilize to contain Peter and prevent him from reaching the dungeon. Word has quickly reached Gordon; he mobilizes every single soldier in the castle to stop Peter. But, the Mark II's has given Peter to ability to breeze through the Legion in the castle with little delay as he tears through the castle to the dungeons.

Meanwhile with Tom and Jamie, they are still waiting in their cell, hearing the sounds of Ultranian gunshots and explosions. The sound of battle is getting louder and louder to them, they whatever is happening outside is getting closer to the them. Jamie leans on the wall while Tom does push-ups to get ready for when Peter arrives. Jamie sees the Dungeon-Master shaking in front of the cell out of fear.

Jamie: What's the matter, Dungeon-Master? Scared?
Dungeon-Master (macho): Me, scared? Bitch, don't make me laugh! I
    am never scared. I come from the toughest parts of Alabama and…
Jamie (out-loud): OH SHIT!

The Dungeon-Master dives on the floor screaming with a scream indistinguishable from a little girl. Jamie begins to laugh, not expecting that he would sound like a girl when he screams.

Dungeon-Master (extremely angry): You know what circus freak, I'm
    sick of your shi…

Dungeon-Master instantly turns white like paper when he sees the entrance to the dungeon blown open and a Legion heavy-gunner flying from it. The Dungeon-Master, shaking from head-to-toe, is pointing his Ultranian shotgun to at the entrance. He then loses all of the pigment in his skin when he sees Peter walk through the entrance of the gate in his slightly damaged Mark II suit. He fires shots at Peter as Peter walk closer towards him. Peter's shields not effected by the shots in the slightest and he does not slow down. He then dashes towards the Dungeon-Master when he needs to reload, grabs him by the neck, holds him up, and pins his head to the cell bars of the Tom and Jamie's cell. Peter is not going to take any of the Dungeon-Master's nonsense.

Peter: Open the cell! Keep resisting, bastard, and you'll end up dead like Omegatronus.

Dungeon-Master: OKAY, OKAY, OKAY… I'll open the cell. Just don't hurt me please. I just shitted on myself.

Peter drops him and he falls on his hands and knees.

Peter: You… are a bitch.

The Dungeon-Master opens Tom and Jamie's cell by pressing the release button on his Warden-Gauntlet. Tom and Jamie walk out of the cell.

Jamie: Freedom at last!

Peter rips the Dungeon-Master's Warden-Gauntlet off, grabs him by the neck, and throws him in the cell. Peter closes the cell on him and destroys the Warden-Gauntlet to permanently lock the cells.

Dungeon-Master (urgency): Hey…! Let me out here! You can't leave me here! The Apex-General or Dark-Knighten will kill me if they find me.

Peter: Be glad we don't kill your ass.

Apex (to Peter): Peter, more Legion soldiers are inbound.

Tom: Something is telling me that we don't have time left.

Peter: Grab on to me and we'll translocate out of here.

Jamie: The sooner the better.

More Legion soldiers storm into the dungeon and prepares to open fire, but Peter instantly translocate when the soldiers arrived. They immediate reappear in the Omega-Star, standing over the Translocator-Cube. The Omega-Star is submerged miles below the surface of the ocean; the Thunderbolts have escaped. A Legion Captain who was in the dungeon contacts Gordon, fearful for his life.

Legion Captain: Uh… Apex-General, sir.

Gordon: Tell me you've captured the Thunderbolt.

Legion Captain (fearful): N…negative sir. He… teleported with the other Thunderbolts.

Gordon: What?!

Legion Captain: They… escaped… sir.

Gordon (outraged): Can't you idiots do anything right?! One job… one fucking job?!

Gordon deactivates his communicator. He thinks about contacting the Legion-Elite to have them find the Thunderbolts, but he realizes that Dark-Knighten will learn of their escape through the Legion-Elites. So he decides to contact every single Military City.

Gordon: Attention all Legion Military Stations, the Thunderbolts have escaped Mundi-Castle. Search the globe and find them before the Dark-Knighten returns. Tom Sullivan, Jamie Kelly, and Peter Orion are wanted alive. I say again; The Thunderbolts are wanted alive.

Legion Soldiers across the planet quickly mobilize and scatter to search and find Tom, Jamie, and Peter. Gordon has officially put the three Thunderbolts on the World's most wanted list, wanted: Alive.

CHAPTER VI

The Grand Exodus

Earth is now on high alert as Gordon mobilized the Peace-Keepers and military soldiers to hunt down the Earth's most wanted three: Tom Sullivan, Jamie Kelly, and Peter Orion. They scatter across the globe as Peace-Keepers march the streets all over the world searching for the three Thunderbolts. They know that if they fail to find them before the Dark-Knighten returns from whatever he is, things will get ugly for them all, especially for Gordon. With this in mind, the entire Legion army has made the capture of fugitives the highest priority of the Earth. However, Gordon refuses the inform the Legion-Elites[45] as each are very close to Dark-Knighten; they would not lie to Dark-Knighten and if Dark-Knighten learns of their escape, Gordon will suffer.

Meanwhile with the Thunderbolts, the Omega-Star is still submerged miles underwater in the dark trenches of the Atlantic. Apex has activated the interior Biotic healing rays in the cargo-bay for the cock-pit for Peter to repair the damage the Mark II has taken.

Apex: We have lost the Legion pursuers.
Tom: In the ocean?

Jamie is in awe as she looks out of the window to see surviving marine life. The Omega-Star flows past a large whale and a large school of fish as life has not yet been destroyed in one place on Earth.

Jamie: How is there still life down here? Those nuclear bombs went off like a week ago? How is the water not contaminated?

---

[45] The Legion's deadliest fighters. Each with skills that rival that of the Thunderbolts.

Apex: It was contaminated until the Legion deployed Denuclearization Satellites created by the Ultranian empire. These satellites orbit a planet, absorb the toxins in the planet and expel it outside of the atmosphere. Leaving no trace.

Tom: How is that even possible?

Peter: It's an Alien Race with tech for installer war and has conquered entire filaments of the universe, Captain. Do you really have to ask?

Tom (Annoyed): Right... Are we able to contact anyone?

Peter talks through the Cargo-Bay's speakers.

Peter: I hate to be the bearer of bad news, but the communications grid is down. The coms center in Magnus was probably destroyed along with everything else.

Jamie: Is that the only thing gone bad?

Peter: The tracking system I have to pin-point the other Thunderbolts is offline. All of their suits must have been damaged, including the tracking systems.

Jamie: Well, that's perfect.

Peter: What's our next move, Captain?

Tom: We need to start by contacting Onyx command to formulate a plan of action and then we find every other Thunderbolts. I need to contact Commander Sullivan.

Jamie: He was in Magnus when it was destroyed, how could we know if he's still alive?

Peter: The same thing can be said for Bridgette, Zack, and the young Turbos. Even my boy, Antonio.

Tom: We won't know unless we figure it out. Peter, I need to use Bridgette's station.

Jamie: How can you use the station without Bridgette being here?

Tom: I can use them.

Peter: Uh, god... We've gone back to hopeless if we're going to need Bridgette's stations.

Jamie (irritated): Don't make come in there and beat you, Anna Mae.

Peter activates the communication station built for Bridgette to use on missions. He instantly gets the reference to the threat.

Peter: Really, Jamie? You want me to eat some cake too?
Jamie (country accent): And you better not never tell nobody but God neither. It'd kill your mama too.
Peter (humored): Jamie, you are something else.

Jamie smirks at Peter's face on the screen knowing that the best thing she can do in keep the Team's Moral up through humor.

Peter: I'll see if I can bring the tracking system back online.

Tom jumps on station and turns it on. Jamie looks at the screen only to see Bridgette's twenty-six password-lock pages and a timer of three minutes. Jamie is completely surprised while Tom expects nothing less because of Bridgette's secretive nature.

Jamie (surprised): Okay, I know that Bridgette doesn't want anyone getting into her secrets, but this is excessive... even for her.

Tom cracks his neck and fingers, then presumes to type and clears all of the twenty-six security pages. He types at a speed nobody has seen beside Bridgette, who has a record of a hundred-fifty words in one minute. Tom's typing speed is not one-fifth of Bridgette's, but he can still go through her passwords. While he swiftly skims though the security passwords, Jamie looks at Tom's hands and is dumbfounded. Jamie has never seen anyone type like this before besides Bridgette; to her, his fingers look like a blur. Tom clears the final page and a an animated simplistic, childish version of Tom appears on the screen, called Cute-Animation. Cute-Tom walks next to a small house with a large bouquet of flowers. He knocks at the door and Cute-Bridgette opens the door, takes the flowers in awe, and kisses Cute-Tom on the cheek. Cute-Tom falls on the ground with his face red and Cute-Bridgette looks at him with blushing. Tom gains access to Bridgette's communication station when the animation finishes. Tom and Jamie did not see the Cute-Animation coming; Tom is confused while Jamie is amazed.

Tom: Okay… uh… I'm in.
Jamie (amazed): Aww Captain, that was adorable.
Tom (blushing): Uh…. let's get back to what we need to do.

Tom uses the station to get into the channel frequency section, which allows Bridgette to hack into any frequency. Jamie thinks of how Bridgette can hack into anything as she looks at Bridgette's monitor.

Jamie: Is this how Bridgette can hack into anything?
Tom: Yeah… but by the time she figures out that I used one of her stations, she will reset every single byte in every single one of her stations. She might even have some of them self-destruct.
Peter: That sounds like something she would do; how paranoid as fuck she is. So, who do you plan to contact first, Captain?
Tom: I need to contact the commander to coordinate a plan of action.
Jamie (doubtful): Hopefully, he's still around.

Tom locates and hacks into a secret communications frequency that only he and Richard know of as this frequency was only used when Tom was six during his training with Richard. But, he sees another hidden frequency connected to his childhood frequency, a two way network. By hacking into the connection of both communication frequencies, Tom has access to both of the frequencies and see the content of the frequencies with ease. It takes a few seconds to hack into the frequencies.

Jamie: By the way, Peter. The Legion took away out battle suits and put them in some storage unit in the castle. You wouldn't happened to come across those, wouldn't you?
Peter: I do. But, they've been critically damaged. I put them in the repair station in the cockpit.
Jamie: Why not put them in the repair station here?

Peter: It just slipped my mind. It'll be repaired in the next three hours.
Jamie: Three hours?!

Meanwhile, under the Magnus Ruins, Richard is on the E.O.M. debating with the Onyx High-Council[46] on a hidden frequency that cannot be tracked or hacked via normal standards. Antonio, on the other hand, is laying down on a rock-bed that he made, annoyed from not being able to go back to sleep. This debate has lasted for three hours; some High-Councilmen refuse to listen to the reason of Richard's argument as he attempts to have them listen to reason. Their debate is so loud, Antonio cannot help but listen even if he plugged his ears. He is commentating silently under his breath while he listens.

Councilman Galloway: Generalissimo, this plan is reckless and it is a
    possibility put Onyx in jeopardy.
Richard: We are on the brink of losing the war. Commencing this
    operation is our only chance of survival and our only chance of
    turning the tide.
Councilmen Talon (outraged): It requires bringing those loose-cannon
    Thunderbolts to Onyx! They will put us all at risk and possibly get
    us all killed.
Antonio: <Chuckles> Our kill count is nowhere near as big as yours.
Richard: If my knowledge is correct, there are five Thunderbolts that
    are currently located in Onyx as we speak. As that correct, Antonio?
Antonio (normal tone): Yes sir. Oz Turbo[47], Sparks Turbo[48], Diane
    Turbo[49], Bridgette Swanson, and Zack Batto. Wherever they are.

---

[46] The Council of Elders who share power with the Generalissimo. Their relationship with the current Generalissimo has grown sour after they defended the actions of the previous Generalissimo and attempted to kill the innocent victims of his horrendous crime.

[47] Fourth oldest member of the Turbo-Family. Ice-Deity. One who has seen too much violence in his life. Caucasian. Ice blue hair. Thick hair. Ice blue eyes. Age 20

[48] Second Youngest member of the Turbo-Family. Speed-Deity. One who finds a reason to move ahead in life. Caucasian. Brown hair. Thick hair. White eyes. Age 18

[49] The Youngest member of the Turbo-Family. "Mana" wielder. One who sees the world in a different force. Pure Pink Eyes. Pink hair. Short hair. Blind. Age 18.

Councilman Talon: Which is far more than necessary. We do not need these failures of Super-Soldiers endangering our planet.

Antonio (silently): No wonder why Peter and Jacob said these guys were bitty old fools who are jealous of young people. I can think of a couple reasons why.

Richard: The Thunderbolt division is the only one that can counter the Legion's deadliest warriors. They are the only one who can win this war for us.

Antonio (silently): That doesn't make us sound like weapons or anything.

Councilman Galloway: They are children with guns and powers. They have never been to war before. We put a lot of resources on them and they still lost the Earth to the Legion. Out of all of the Super-Soldier Programs we have created, the Thunderbolts are the biggest failures. A clear result of sending kids to do an adult's job.

Antonio (silently): I want to see him do better. He needs to get some fiber first.

Councilman Tenzin: We're wasting time with this meaningless argument. We are at war and we cannot leave any Onyx behind. Regardless if you think that the Thunderbolts are reckless, they are still our soldiers, valuable soldiers at that. Leaving them behind will do far more harm than good.

Councilwoman Kensington: I second that notion. We need to bring the Thunderbolts to Onyx in order to form a new plan of attack and this operation is our only means to do either one.

Councilman Galloway: This will bring more risk than gain.

Councilman Reyes: This is a risk that we have no other alternative but to take, Galloway. But, Generalissimo Sullivan, the only question I have is how do you intend to commence this plan. You will need to activate the teleportation drives across Magnus, contact all Thunderbolts across the planet, and bring them into the city of Magnus. How do you intend to meet all of these...

Richard and the High-Council both see an anomaly on their communications frequency.

Richard: I'm getting an anomaly.

Councilman Galloway: How is that possible? This is a highly secured channel that cannot be hacked!

Antonio (silently): You must be the love-child of a brain-damaged horse and a bucket of its own shit if you believe that crap while knowing who Bridgette is. Bridgette must be better than they say she is.

Cute-Bridgette falls into the screen from the top. She laughs at them and says, "You've been hacked." Static shows up on the E.O.M. and Richard, along with the High-Council, sees Tom's face on the frequency.

Richard (shocked): Tom, is that you?

Antonio: Tom? The Captain?

Councilman Talon: How did you hack into this frequency?

Tom: That information is on a need-to-know basic, Councilman. Irrelevant as well.

Councilman Talon feels like he is sensing insubordination.

Councilman Talon: Why you isolate little…

Councilman Reyes: How do we know if you are the real Tom Sullivan?

Tom whistles a song that he and Richard used to whistle to say when a simulated mission commences or complete, "Mary had a little lamb." As Richard finishes hearing the song, he automatically knows that this is the real Tom. Richard begins to shed a tear down one of his eyes after visualizing memories of Tom when he was a little boy.

Richard (relieved): That's the real Captain Sullivan. I taught him that song when he was three years old.

Tom: Do you have a tear running down your eye, commander?

Richard (to Tom): Sorry. <clears throat> What is your status, Captain?

Tom: I am accompanied by Agent Kelly and Agent Orion. We have just recently managed to escape Mundi Castle.

Richard: Agent Knighten and Agent Shulls went to Mundi Castle to assassinate the Dark-Knighten if I'm not mistaken. What is the status on those two?

Tom: Agent Knighten is K.I.A, commander. Agent Shulls was nowhere to be detected in Mundi Castle. They could not stop the Dark-Knighten and Agent Knighten's death could've possibly affected Dark-Knighten mentally.

Richard (regret): K.I.A, huh… <Sigh> That is to be expected, Agent Knighten and Dark-Knighten are twins. What is your location, Captain?

Tom: Under the Atlantic Ocean… Long story. We plan to find more surviving Thunderbolts to to come up with a plan of attack…

Councilman Talon (condescending): Excuse me… Can we please go back to our original conversation before we were so rudely interrupted.

Jamie (to herself): Pot calling the cattle "black."

Richard: Councilman Talon, we were in the middle of a debrief in the situation beyond the city limits.

Tom: The war is not going in our favor, Councilman. With no leadership, the Onyx forces have been scattered across the planet with no direct, no strategy. Our communications system is down. The Legion knew that attacking Magnus was the ultimate means getting the edge against us. All Onyx, and even Thunderbolt, forces are either dead, captured, or missing.

Richard: In addition, Councilman Talon, Legion Soldiers are marching across Magnus searching for survivors.

Peter: How heavily guarded is Magnus?

Richard: According to Agent A. Turbo, there are Legion fighters and tanks scattered across the ruined streets with heavily-armed soldiers marching the streets?

Jamie: Commander Sullivan, how did you manage to escape the blast?

Antonio: I saved him at the last second before the laser vaporized the plaza!

Peter (happy): Is that you, Antonio?! Man, I thought they got your ass.

Antonio: Shit…, listening to these the commander bicker with these old men 'cause they want to leave us Thunderbolts to die, I wish they did.

Jamie: What?

Peter: You're kidding me.

Antonio: Oh, I shit you not. These old-ass mother-fuckers want to leave us to die out here. Calling us failures and kids with guns and all that shit.

Councilman Galloway: This is what I mean. The Thunderbolts are immature and unprofessional children and placing all of our hope into these kids will lead to our downfall.

Tom (to Galloway): Regardless of how you think about us, and to be blunt, we are all you have.

Jamie (to Galloway): You should be glad that we're still fighting for all of you. After McAllen.

Richard has had enough of this conversation with the High-Council.

Richard: I've heard enough. High-Council, I am disconnecting to commence the operation. I expect you to have the warp-gate to Onyx ready when I give the signal to activate it. There will be hell to pay if you don't commence the operation.

Richard cuts the feed to the High-Council to talk specifically to Tom.

Tom: Do you have a plan, Commander?

Richard: I do. I've commenced a full scale retreat "Exodus Protocol".
      Gather as many Thunderbolts as you can and report back to me.

Tom: Yes sir. Captain Sullivan out.

The feed between Tom and Richard cuts off. Richard closes the E.O.M. and turns his attention to Antonio.

Richard: Antonio, I need you to reactivate the generators underneath the city.

Antonio: "Generators underneath the city," Commander?

Richard: I take it you can use your Terra-Powers to sense the generators' locations.

Antonio: I can only sense an underground bunker about two miles underground and... Right...

Richard: Go to the nearest generator and contact me when you get there.

Antonio: Yes sir.

Antonio puts his hand on the ground to sense where to find the bunker, gets the location, and Terra-Swims to it.

Richard uses the E.O.M. to initiate the full scale retreat operation: The Exodus Protocol. Tom deactivates Bridgette's station.

Peter: At least we have a plan now. But, one problem... how do we find our guys?

Tom: I overheard some guards before we went to Mundi Castle and they said the Legion deployed a special task unit to suppress and subjugate the populace called the Peacekeepers. They're keeping surveillance for any signs of resistance. If we can tap into their data banks, we should be able to get info on where they are.

Jamie: Peter, how much time do have until those suits are repaired.

Peter: Another two hours and fifty minutes. What do we do in the mean time?

Tom: Just stay underwater until those suits are fully repaired.

Peter: How come we don't just hack our way into the Peacekeeper files from here?

Tom: For all we know, they may have a way to track any hacker and pinpoint their locations.

Peter: So much for it being easy.

Jamie: Well at least we get a break. Hey Peter, didn't those suits also have those jumpsuits inside.

Peter: Sorry Jamie, but no. I didn't get that lucky.

Jamie (disappointed): Dammit… this prison suit is starting to give me a bad itch. Plus, it has a bunch of blood on it with most of it not being my own.

Tom: How do you get somebody else's blood on your outfit?

Jamie: I had a lot of people who tried to rape me in those prison; I had to fight and nearly kill them all.

Tom: Ugh… Forget I asked.

Chapter VII
Cruel World

Legion Peacekeepers have established a fortress of operations in the middle of the Denver-Ruins as the Legion-City finishes its fortifications. Three hundred miles away from the Legion-City and inside the Denver-Ruins, this fortress is built to suppress any populace who managed to survive the nuclear fallout. Peacekeepers drop in by aircraft and drop-ship and they march the streets of the Denver-Ruins searching for survivors of the destruction to provide shelter and rebels to irradiate. Denver is one of the most observed cities on Earth because it is where Thunderbolts: Kendall Knighten Jr., Kylie Shulls, Zackery Bato, Dominic Thomas, and Sheila Warrens grew up and Legion commanders suspect they may be close to home. The traitorous Road-Vipers have informed the Peacekeepers about Beth and Kylie's presence in Denver, bringing in Military personnel that are to inform Gordon of Kylie's capture. The Peacekeepers are heavily armed and extremely dangerous and; they believe they are prepared for everything. However, the Peacekeepers are being watched by Beth with her E.C. sniper rifle scope on a rooftop. She has her sights on a Legion Caravan packed full of explosives with her EC scope that can see through the dark, blinding ash-covered winds. Beth has a Tele-Link to contact Kylie.

Beth: Kylie, how's it going on your end?
Kylie: I have my sights on a straggler. I'm moving in to get his outfit.
Beth: Let's hurry this up. These pieces of shit are brea.

Kylie takes a deep breath as she uses her Energy Core to activate her E.C. Build[50] in order to increase her attributes. She stands inside of the remains of a destroyed building, watching the straggler. She can see that the straggler is shaking in his armor as he knows that a Thunderbolt is in the city and he's heard stories of a single Thunderbolt being able to take down an entire battalions by themselves. Kylie sees the fear in the straggler, jumps down in front of the straggler, and scares the straggler. He falls on the ground looking up to Kylie. He gets up and throws a punch at Kylie; she blocks it the punch and presses the button on his converter to drop his suit. She punches the straggler in the nose, puts her hands on his head, and snaps his neck. Kylie, with no speck of sweat broken, contacts Beth.

Kylie: Alright, I found a good disguise.
Beth: Good, let's keep going.
Kylie: I infiltrate the fortress and disable the fortress's defenses while
    you provide a distraction to their forces.
Beth: Let me know if any civilians are inside. What I have in mind will
    do some serious collateral damage.
Kylie: Just let me know ahead of time so I can get in the clear.
Beth: Can do. Beth out.

Kylie converts her suit into it's stealth mode in the form of a gauntlet and sees her Tele-Link dissipate off her left arm. Kylie places the Legion converter on her left arm, converts it into its Battle-Suit mode that adjusted to her female figure, picks up the gun that the straggler had, and heads for the base.

Meanwhile with Beth, she is on the second floor with the caravan in her sights. She also sees that one of her former Road-Viper lieutenants, Cobra riding in front of the caravan. Looking at Cobra's face, Beth can remember how she used to play with Cobra when she was little, they

---

[50] An E.C. technique that allows the user to use their Energy Core to increase her attributes. Due to Kylie's years of training and experience as Safe-Guardian, she has mastered numerous techniques and even taught what she knows to Beth, Kendall, Zach, Dom, Sheila, and Christina.

played games like mock Sumo-Wrestling as Cobra has a large bulge of a belly when Beth was little, he is the one who taught her how to use pistols and explosives, he even helped Beth get ready for school dances with her friends, even Prom. She also remembers how he was the one who tried to knock her out and he spat in her face after they sold her out. Beth knows that she can simply kill him with a headshot, but she decides not to. Beth knows what she has to do to her old friend; she shots and blows his front tire, causing him to whip-out off the road. The driver of the Caravan stops to help Cobra. Beth relocates.

Cobra crawls away from his destroyed motorcycle; Peacekeepers walk up to him and force him up.

Peacekeeper 1: What are you doing?

Cobra: My tire blew out.

Caravan driver: Why do we have to have you ride with us?

Cobra: The captain agreed to let us join the Legion if we help you find Beth and her Thunderbolt friend.

Caravan Driver: Oooooh…. let me bring out the red carpet for you and your dirt-bag bikers. I'm seriously astonished in how you were able to sell out your old boss.

Cobra: She was leading us down to being community service punks. Here I thought we didn't raise a punk-bitch.

Caravan Driver: I wouldn't want sell outs like you in our…

The Caravan Driver get headshot from the back of his head; he even watched the E.C. Bullet fly from the back of his head into the ground. The Caravan Driver stands for a few seconds before falling forward dead. Cobra is standing stiff like a deer in headlights; he gets shot in the leg and screams in pain. He falls onto the ground with tears from his eye, in agony as the E.C. bullet, indistinguishable from normal bullets and dissipate on impact with the ground, went through a couple of nerves.

Beth: "Punk-Bitch," huh?

Cobra recognizes Beth's voice and looks behind him to see Beth standing behind her with her mask off. Cobra is so afraid, his face goes completely pale.

Cobra (abject fear): B-B-Beth... uh... what are you doing here?

Beth: I'm guessing being in the Legion for like a half a week and all this ash and debris made you dumber. It should be clear what I'm doing here.

Cobra: <Groan> You... you're hear to kill me, aren't you?

Beth: I guess you grew a brain being around that Alien tech.... You know, I knew you were on the slow side, even slower than Kendall was and he has Asperger's. But, I never thought I would see the day that people who considered my family would betray me. You lead me to an ambush spot and tried to have Legion soldiers gun me down. You, Cobra, knock me down and spit in my face before they tried to kill me. Too bad for you I managed to escape.

Cobra: Beth, you...

Beth (furious): SHUT UP!!!

Cobra quickly shuts his mouth, seeing the rage in her eyes.

Beth: I can't believe it, honestly. I defended you guys from my friends every day up to Graduation. "Don't go with them, Beth," "They'll get you killed, Beth," "They're a bunch of psychos," "Low-life dirty scumbags who are better off locked up." I defended you guys and kept you all from getting in the prison yard and graveyard because you were my family. You raised me after my parents were poisoned by the Vices; you were my family and I loved each and every single one of you like family... and you sold me out. Why, Cobra? I used to take naps on fat-belly up until I was five. How could you do this to me?

Cobra: You really want to know why?

Beth shots Cobra in both kneecaps, making him scream in the pain. Cobra asked that to irritate Beth; Beth knew this and that's why she decided to shot him.

Beth: Talk!

Cobra: Listen Titanoboa... Beth, you've turned the Road-Vipers from the most feared gang in all states of the Rocky Mountains into a pussy-ass public service group. Helping people and shit, not doing what we were meant to do: riding down the highway to Hell. You made us trade all of our cocks into pussies.

Beth: Are you fucking serious? So trying to lead the Road-Vipers on a new path where people would actually like us is a bad thing? To no longer seem like a bunch of criminals? I can't believe I actually thought I saw something good inside of you guys.

Cobra: You were delusional, Beth. I loved you like a niece and I wanted you to be tough, but those friends of yours made you soft. You were never fit to have the name, Titanoboa.

Beth walks up to Cobra and places the barrel up to his chin.

Beth: Maybe I was delusional for seeing a future for the Road-Vipers.

Beth, with tears in her eyes, pulls the trigger and blows Cobra's brains out of the top of his skull. She dissipates the gun and sees that she has killed a man that she saw as a big brother. She drops down to her knees with tears running down her face and starts resisting to cry. Beth knew that she had to kill him, but deep down, she did not want. She sees streams of tears fall in the ashes on the ground as the Tele-Link appears on her arm.

Kylie: Beth, I'm inside of the fortress. I'm heading for the security room.

Beth (sad): Yeah...

Kylie: Beth, what's wrong?

Beth (Saddened): I had my sights on Cobra. I... I...

Kylie (sympathetic): Beth...

Beth (saddened): I killed him. I had to kill somebody who was like a brother to me.

Kylie (sympathetic): Beth, I'm so sorry to hear that… I know how much he meant to you. But, think about it… it was either you or him. If you didn't kill him, then he still would've killed you or at least tried to. I know that he was close to you, in fact I thought that he was a nice guy. Slow, but nice. But, it had to be done.

Beth: Kylie…

Kylie: Again, I'm sorry, Beth. But deep down…, you know I'm right.

Beth: <Sigh> Yeah. Are there any civilians inside of the fortress?

Kylie: No… they're not even looking for a single civilian. You're clear to go for whatever you plan to do.

Beth: Yeah, these bastards are going to pay for stabbing me in the back. Beth out.

The Tele-Link dissipates as Kylie reaches the Security-Room; she looks around to see that there are no Legion soldiers nearby. She approaches the door and sees that she needs an Ultranian access code to get inside. Kylie doesn't have an access code; so she directs her EC energy into her hand, presses her hand on the console, and uses her energy to override the security systems to open the door. She quickly moves inside as the door closes behind her. The Security-Room is completely dark with the only light in the room coming from the monitors. The Security Manager is leaned back in his chair with his feet next to the keypad for the monitors with a box of donuts on his bloated stomach with sprinkles and jelly stains on his uniform. He belches and puts the donuts aside after he hears the doors open and close.

Security Manager (impatient): It's about time you came back. Hand over the coffee, pipsqueak.

Kylie sneaks behind the Security Manager, silently conjures her normal E.C. sword, and rams the sword behind the chair and through the Security Manager's heart, killing him instantly. Kylie dissipate the sword while it is still hanging inside of the Security Manager. Kylie can her approaching footsteps and moves to the dark corner of the room next to the door where she cannot be seen. The door opens; Kylie conjures her sword again as the Legion soldier walks in with coffee. Before the soldier notices the dead body of the security manager, Kylie rams her sword in the soldier's head and goes through his brain, killing him instantly. Kylie dissipates his sword while inside the soldier's head; the soldier falls to the side and drops the coffee. Kylie closes and locks the door so nobody else can walk inside. She pushes the chair with the dead Security Manager to the side and gets ready to type on the monitor. Kylie presumes to deactivate the security systems and activates a Tele-link with Beth.

Kylie: Okay Beth, I'm disabling the security systems and the alarm. How are things in your end?
Beth: I'm getting ready to start that distraction now.

Kylie finishes deactivating the security systems.

Kylie: Alright, I need to make it to the archives room. What exactly do you plan to do?

Beth does not respond.

Kylie: Beth…? Beth!

Kylie looks at the security feed in the front of the Fortress and she sees a Caravan racing straight into the heart of the fortress. What Kylie does not realize is that Beth is driving the Caravan with every single explosive inside armed to detonate. When she gets close to the blockade, she ejects from the caravan and watches it crash and create a large explosion with a shockwave that can be felt throughout the entire fortress and an explosion so massive, it whips out most of the Legion in the courtyard of the base.

Kylie: Beth…! I didn't finish deactivating the defenses.

Beth (determined): I don't care. I'm bringing all of these bastards out here. The Road-Vipers die now.

Beth dissipate the Tele-Link.

Kylie: Beth? Beth…! Goddamnit! <Sigh> I gotta do this the old fashioned way.

Kylie deactivate her Legion disguise and takes off the Legion gauntlet to throw it to the side. She activates her Thunderbolt Suit converter to go from stealth-mode to battle mode. She conjures a missile launcher on the assault rifle for extra fire-power top as she hears Legion soldiers outside of the room; she uses a shockwave to blow the door and go through the soldiers in front of her. The E.C. powered projectiles eliminate the soldiers in her way, giving Kylie a chance to make a break to the AA-Gun controls with her Velocity-Boots fully charged. The Velocity-Boots allow her to run faster than any normal human and as fast as the speed of sound at max-power. Kylie can move so fast with those boots, she can run on walls and even the ceiling. She uses short burst of the Velocity-Boots to move through the soldiers.

She tears through the hallways, guns down any Legion soldiers that get in her way using her E.C. powered weapons which is more than capable of killing Ultranians along with any other race in existence. She was trained in the ways of the ancient order of the Mystic Safe-Guardians ever since she was five, mastering several forms of Martial Arts and the use of multiple weapons. Any obstacles that would get in Kylie's way, even when her Velocity-Boots would run out of power or if Legion soldiers would surround her, gets destroyed and she would eliminate the soldiers by the dozens. Kylie eventually reaches the Controls for the fortress's defenses and conjures her E.C. Pistols and gets ready to destroy the controls.

Meanwhile with Beth, she rides on her E.C. Motorcycle and two fighter-jets. She conjures massive guns on the back of her motorcycle that automatically fires at the jets. Beth makes a sharp turn and sees a large Legion truck charging straight at her; Beth decides to play chicken.

Beth speeds up straight into the truck; the driver of the truck goes fun force towards Beth. The truck is moving with five times the force of a freight train. When they are thirty meters away, Beth jumps off the motorcycle to make it dissipate; she recovers with a roll and punches the truck full force; the truck's back leads into the air and the truck flies into the fighter-jets to destroy all three of them. Beth conjures high-powered E.C. Pistols, activates her E.C. Build, and opens fire on the swarming ships around her. These Ultranian Fighter-Jets were built to withstand the force of meteors as they were built for interstellar war, but Beth's E.C. Powered bullets are strong enough to blow through their armored plating. Legion Fighter-Jets are getting shot down and are crashing into the ground and the buildings around Beth. The ashes, dust, and debris are blowing out of control, but even these are not slowing Beth as her mask is protecting her eyes. The Fighter-Jets are trying to gun her down, but Beth speed and reflexes have been enhanced through the E.C. Build and she counterstrikes by shooting them out of the sky. A Legion Drop-ship hovers behind her with a charging gatling-gun. Beth hears the drop-ship and turns around with an E.C. R.P.G. and fires an E.C. Powered rocket into the engine and destroys it, sending the drop-ship to fall into the next building and explode on impact. Beth sees that the Road-Vipers are not out there trying to fight her and she gets mad. While fighting, she contacts Kylie with the Tele-Link.

Beth: Kylie, those bastards aren't out here.
Kylie: Maybe it's because they see fighting off a fleet of Legion jets and winning.
Beth: Urgh…! They must be hiding inside. See if you can find them.
   If you do, leave Rattlesnake alive. His ass is mine.
Kylie: Got it.

Kylie finished destroying the last of the controls, deactivating the AA-Guns. She then make her way through the chaos-ridden fortress in search of the Road-Vipers. She goes to the Launching-Station, where the airships are located, and sees the Road-Vipers, lead by Rattlesnake[51], trying to escape. Kylie drops down into the launching station with her Elemental-Sword on fire and runs towards them with her E.C. Build activated. They see her and they open fire on her, she reflects their fire directly back at them; the fire goes back into the Road-Viper through their chests or their heads. Kylie focuses fire energy to the tip of her sword and she slashes his sword to create a sword beam into the engines of the drop-ship they trying to board. The Road-Vipers scatter as they will be killed by the explosion; Kylie switch the energy to wind and fires a stream of wind out of her hand and blows the drop-ship back before it explodes. Kylie them switches to Lightning and dashes to the Road-Vipers to slash them; one after another fell to her sword. Rattlesnake was all that was left; Kylie dashes to him and kicks him in the face, knocking him out without knocking his head off.

Kylie: You jerks had it coming.

Kylie conjures the Tele-Link and contacts Beth.

Kylie: Beth, I found the Road-Vipers. They were trying to escape.
Beth: Did you kill them?
Kylie: I had to or else they would've escaped. I left Rattlesnake alive for you.
Beth: Perfect… I'll be right over. Uhh… where are you exactly?
Kylie: In the back of the base.

Beth dissipates the Tele-Link on the top of a flying Legion Fighter-Jet, blasting more Fighter-Jets and Aerial-Troopers who were chasing her. Beth thinks of a way to get back into street-level; she decides the shoot the engines of the jet to cause it to crash. She fires on the engines on the jet and rams her fingers through the armor of the ship as it falls. The wind is blowing in Beth's face; she waits until she was about thirty

---

[51] Beth's former Lieutenant. A big brother to her. Somebody who's been a mentor to her. He was the one who taught her how to keep a boy happy while she used to date Zack. He used to scare Zack like a father would on the first date.

feet off the ground to jump. She conjures her motorcycle mid-air and drops back down to the street on her bike, unfazed. She rides through the blazing fortress with her large bike guns as Legion forces retreat. She would blast holes through the walls to ride through the fortress. She stops right in front of Kylie and Rattlesnake. Kylie switches the Elemental-Sword's energy into water to have water fall into his face to have him regain consciousness. He sees Kylie and Beth standing over him; Kylie is indifferent to whatever happens him and Beth has every intent to killing him, despite how much she does not want to.

Beth conjures her EC-Pistols and aims it directly at Rattlesnake's face. Rattlesnake holds his bloody nose while he looks up to see the fire in Beth's eyes in the rampaged fortress. Rattlesnake sees that it all backfired and he wants to get back into Beth's good graces.

Rattlesnake: B-B-Beth… Beth! Wait a minute!

Beth: Don't try to weasel your way out of this, motherfucker. You'll only delay the inevitable.

Rattlesnake: We were only trying to bring back the proud name of the Road-Vipers. We were supposed to ride the…

Beth: Rocky Mountains as the most feared biker gang. Yeah, that what Cobra said. Do you seriously believe that our ride would last forever?

Rattlesnake tries to answer, but Beth cuts him off.

Beth: Stop…. I know that you realized that shit hit the fan and instead of us staying together, you just threw me under the bus. After you raised me, took care of me after the Vices killed my parents. You even fought alongside me, Kylie, and the rest of my friends. We've been through the most of it all and you just turn on me.

Rattlesnake sees the tears in Beth's eyes and he family sees that what he has done is wrong. He sees that he hurt somebody who looked up to him and he gets sincere.

Rattlesnake (apologetic): Bethlehem, all we wanted was to restore the proud name of the Road-Vipers. We were not meant to be the heroes or saviors. We were a gang that has been outcast by the world. Your family started this gang to give us outcasts a chance to get back at the world that deserted us. This is just who we are.

Beth: We didn't have to live the life of psychopaths or outcast, we could've been better than that. We could've had a better purpose in life that actually had better meaning than revenge and hatred. We could've been something beneficial to the world. But no..., when things went downhill, you just give up and join the ones who sold out the humanity. You *were* my family, but not anymore. You're just a bunch of psychopaths that I don't even know anymore. Nothing personal, right?

Rattlesnake: Beth, WAIT!!! DON'T...

Beth closes her eyes to not see Rattlesnake die by her hands as she shots him in the head. She opens her eyes to see Rattlesnake's lifeless body laying on the floor. Kylie can clearly see that all of this is extremely hard on Beth; she raps her arm around Beth's shoulder to comfort Beth. Returning the favor for the kindness Beth has constantly given her.

Kylie: I'm sorry this happened, Beth. I know this couldn't have been easy.

Beth: <Sigh> Believe me... it wasn't. But, it had to be done. The Road-Vipers is dead now. I see this as shedding my skin.

Beth, with lingering sorrow, grabs the Road-Viper symbol on her jacket near her shoulder and tears it off. She looks at the Dead-Eyed Snake Head in her hand, crumbles it up, and lets it go. Kylie watches, knowing how symbolic it is for her. The symbolism comes to an end when they see a Jumbotron turn on with Gordon's face on a two-way feed.

Gordon: Well, well... look at this. Janet's little Thunderbolt sister reappears.

Beth: Kylie, who is that?

Kylie: The Apex-General… the highest ranking general in the entire Legion.

Gordon: I had a feeling that some of you Thunderbolts would be close to home. Fitting how I'd find you and a friend of yours after what happened to the Dark-Knighten's older brother.

Kylie realizes that he is talking about Kendall.

Kylie: What are you talking about?

Gordon: You and that boy made a real mess of this ancient castle to find the Dark-Knighten. I've never seen the amount of raw power he had in any other deity I've seen, not even the Brotherhood-of-Gods in Kinto had that kind of power. But in the end, it wasn't enough.

Beth: Wait, wait, wait, wait… what are you saying old man?

Gordon: That boy, Kendall was his name I think, died fighting the Dark-Knighten.

Kylie and Beth are utterly speechless as they heard what they just heard. Kylie gets on her hands and knee in pure despair while Beth is in complete anger and denial. Gordon feels zero remorse for breaking the news to his enemies.

Beth: You're lying… YOU'RE LYING!!!

Gordon: I usually hate to break this type of news to people, but how you Thunderbolts have constantly made a fool of me as this war has progressed. You receive no sympathy from me… not anymore, even though you're young.

Beth (furious): You son of a bitch!

Gordon: I wouldn't feel sad about your friend. You'll be joining him soon.

Legion Soldiers rush inside of the Launching-Station as a Legion Warship is approaching the Fortress. The soldiers are armed and aiming directly at Kylie and Beth; Beth is ready to fight, but Kylie is too saddened to fight. Beth urges Kylie to get up and fight.

Beth: Kylie, get up! Come on, girl. Get up!
Gordon: <Laugh> If only Sullivan can see the writing on the wall. You
    Thunderbolts have lost and all of you will die...

    The Jumbotron is destroyed by repulser sniper bullet. Kylie and Beth see this and they don't know what happened. The Legion soldiers open fire on Kylie and Beth, but an Ultranian-Barrier is projected in front of the two and the repulser fire is blocked. Beth has no idea what's happening, but Kylie does. The Legion soldiers get caught of guard when the see Jamie in the distance with her personal sniper rifle, the Phantom-Maker, getting head-shots on the Legions soldiers. They scatter as Jamie is sniping them; this exactly what Jamie wants them to do as Tom sprints in behind them as he activates Smart-Sights[52] and guns down the rest of the Legion who try to avoid the fire, the repulsers simply seek them out. Beth has no idea who they are; Kylie, on the other hand, is relieved to see that the cavalry has arrived. She is relieved that she is not alone.

Tom: Kylie, are you alright?
Kylie (relieved): Captain Sullivan... Jamie... you two are alive!
Jamie: You honestly believe that they can kill us. We're Thunderbolts.
    Take more than this to kill us.
Kylie: How did you find us?
Jamie: We taped into their communications and data base. They were
    searching for you in Denver. So we came here knowing we'd find you.
Beth: Wait a minute... what are you guys?
Jamie: Who are you?
Tom: Let's put the introductions on hold for now. Peter, did you find
    any ammunition in this fortress.

---

[52] Once synchronized with any gun, this aims for the user. It causes the bullet to go into the target and the user does not have to aim, only fire.

Peter: Yes sir. This place is completely recked, but the ammo hasn't been touched.

Tom: Good, now let's hurry and get out of here.

Tom directs his attention to Beth. He does not know her, but he can tell that she is a friend of Kylie and Kylie has very powerful friends.

Tom: I don't know who you are, but you seem like one of Kylie's friends.

Kylie: She is, Captain. Her name is Beth and she grew up with me, Sheila, Kendall, Zack, and Dom. I taught her the same thing that I taught the others.

Jamie: If the two of you did all of this damage, then we can definitely use the extra help in the fight.

Kylie: Exactly, Beth can be a valuable new member of the Thunderbolts.

Beth: Wait, wait, wait… this all so sudden and out of no where.

Tom: I'm sorry for the sudden question, Beth. But, we're short on time. So I'm have to be blunt. Will you join the Thunderbolts?

Beth thinks about it and she thinks about how she has nothing left now and she actually has a chance to see her old friends again.

Beth: Friends of Kylie are friends of mine. Count me in.

Tom: Alright then. Peter, get us out of here.

Peter: Roger that.

Peter gets inside of the cockpit after raiding the fortress for ammunition and takes control of the Omega-Star. He flies into the Launching-Station and lands near the Thunderbolts. Tom and Kylie make their way into the Omega-Star as Beth looks at Rattlesnake's dead body. Jamie gets her attention before getting inside of the Omega-Star.

Jamie: Welcome to the team, Beth.

Beth looks down at the Rattlesnake and realizes that she could not make something new out of her old life and has to leave it behind to truly start anew. She runs inside of the Omega-Star. Peter fires out up the engine and blasts off into the skies for everyone to see Gordon's personal warship is approaching the Denver-Ruins. Gordon's ship has a visual on the Omega-Star and orders his crew to open fire. But, little do they know, Peter activated the Omega-Star's Warp-Drive engines and the Omega-Star warps out their detection range.

Gordon realizes that the Thunderbolts have escaped again and screams out of frustration and anger.

Gordon (angry): Goddammit!

Gordon Personal attendant: Apex-General. Why not just contact the Legion-Elites. The Thunderbolts have been weakened and the Legion-Elites have gotten stronger. They can catch the Thunderbolts no problem.

Gordon (frustrated): I'm going to tell you this one final time before I shoot you in the face. If they were involved, then Dark-Knighten will realize what happened and my ass will be grass. We must capture them without the Elites...

Gordon gets an realization and develops an idea of how he will do that, using a weakness that Tom might have.

Gordon (smug): And I think I know just how to do that.

CHAPTER VIII
The Unexpected

The Omega-Star warps into the clouds over the Toronto-Ruins in the stratosphere, escaping Gordon's reach. Beth and Jamie are confused with what just happened. Kylie is relieved that she and Beth made it out, but is still upset in what happened to Kendall. Tom gets back on the Communication-Station. Peter checks the warp-drive and sees that its cool down is another twelve hours.

Jamie (concerned): Peter, what was that?

Peter: Warp-Drive. Just out of the prototype phase, but its cool down is half a day.

Jamie: Well, that sucks.

Peter: You're telling me. What if we run into Gordon again?

Jamie: We'll may have to actually take him out when we get the chance.

Tom: Don't worry, we'll get our chance and when it presents itself, the Apex-General will die.

Jamie: After all the things he's done to Deity-kind, his death is so overdue.

Beth: Can I ask you guys something? How did you manage to find us.

Bridgette: They had help.

Beth: The fuck?

Beth sees Bridgette Swanson's face on the Communication-Station as Bridgette hacked into it. Beth does not know what to think as she's seen numerous alien machines all over the planet.

Beth: Uh… is she a lady in the computer? Like those A.I. things?

Jamie: No, she's a human like the rest of us. Her name's Bridgette. She's practically the World's Greatest Hacker.

Bridgette (appreciative): Thank you, Jamie.

Jamie: And she's also a kill count of 347 with an old Junker Laptop.

Beth: Damn.

Bridgette (emotionless): Thanks, Jamie.

Tom: Alright then, introductions are out of the way. Bridgette, How are you contacting us?

Bridgette: Captain, you forget I can hack into my Stations?

Tom: Ok, let me rephrase that question... why are you contacting us?

Bridgette: I'm here to give you the locations of all of the remaining Thunderbolts on Earth.

Peter: How can you do that? Their Trackers are down.

Bridgette: I instilled secondary trackers inside of your bodies. Remember the banquet we all had. I put the trackers inside the food that would fuse into your necks.

Jamie: You put Trackers in us?

Tom: We'll talk about that later... how many Thunderbolts can you pinpoint?

Bridgette: Only two, Captain. Jack and Agent-Thomas.

Kylie: Captain, do you seriously think we should get Agent-Thomas. after what he's done.

Peter: I agree with Kylie. He nearly got each of us killed more times than I can count. I say we should simply leave him to the wolves.

Tom: I don't trust Agent-Thomas no more than everyone else, but we need to keep him around and alive as ordered by the High-Council. If anything happens to him, then we may some hell to pay.

Jamie: We have to keep him alive.

Tom: Unfortunately.

Peter: Well, let's not waste time. Agent-Thomas's location is closest.

Tom: Well, let's get going.

The Omega-Star flies towards the clouded and soon to be snowy skies forest surrounding the Onyx Nuclear-Base: Zodiac, which have gone through a meltdown. Peter has Apex scanning for Agent-Thomas's signal. However, Apex is having difficulties pin-pointing his signal as the malfunctioning Signal-Jammers inside Zodiac go haywire.

Peter: Apex, did you pin-point the Agent-Thomas's signal yet?

Apex: There's massive interference in this area. I cannot find Agent-Thomas's signal under it all.

Peter (annoyed): It's never that easy. Captain, Apex can't pin-point Agent-Thomas's signal. He said there's too much interference in the area.

Tom: Highlight the area where his signal was last detected. Jamie and I will have to search on foot.

Jamie sees the highlighted area on her holomap and is astonished.

Peter: Yes sir.

The Omega-Star hovers near the Nuclear-Base: Zodiac. Tom and Jamie load up with their gear repaired.

Tom: Peter, keep to the skies and make sure no Legion ships followed us.

Peter: I'm all over it.

Tom (to Jamie): Ready, Jamie?

Jamie: Always.

Tom: Let's go!

Tom and Jamie jump out of the Omega-Star and watch the Cargo-Bay doors close behind them. Peter fires the engine to have the Omega-Star launch and fly over the entire forest. Tom activates the communications channel to the Omega-Star.

Tom (to Peter): Try to see if you can clear up the signal in the air.

Peter: I'll see if I can, but from the looks of the signal jamming, there's no guaranties. Try taking out the jammers, that should clear out all of the interference.

Tom: Mark the source of the inference and we'll take out the jammers.

Peter: Jammers marked. Good hunting, you two. Try not to have too much fun without me.

Jamie: Trust me, Peter, there's nothing fun here but snow for snowman or snow-angels.

Peter: I can see that.

Tom and Jamie see the signal of the jammers on the holomap is inside of the Nuclear-Base. Tom and Jamie make their way to the Base, but their movement speed is severely cut with snow on the ground reaching to their waists. Tom leads the way to the base as he cuts through the snow, but Jamie is struggling to keep up. Seeing that she is beginning to fall behind, Jamie fires her grappling hook at a tree branch that can support her weight and grapples to the tree branch. When Jamie lands on the branch, snow falls from it and on the ground, getting Tom's attention. Tom looks up to see Jamie looking down on him from a tree branch.

Jamie: I can move to the base faster this way.

Tom: Good idea. You deal with those jammers while I'll stay here. We might be closer to Agent Thomas than we think.

Jamie utilizes her grappling hooks and her advanced agility to move through the trees towards the signal jammers. When Jamie reaches the Zodiac, the optics in her helmet begin to get so much static, she cannot see through her helmet. The static causes discomfort to Jamie's eyes, making her disassemble her helmet. She rubs her eyes out of natural reflex and she turns on her communicator to contact the others.

Jamie: I'm inside the base, those jammers are messing with the optics in my helmet.

Tom: Just hurry and get those jammers. My Smart-Sight's detection systems are jammed so I cannot Agent Thomas's signal with it. The sooner we get out of here, the better.

Jamie: Roger that.

Jamie activates the detection system in her left arm in order to pinpoint where the jamming signal is at its strongest and makes her way to where the signal is stronger. As she moves through Zodiac, she can see the damage done inside. There is no light inside of the destroyed Zodiac and most of the walls are blown with massive holes big enough for pachyderms fit through. There are Onyx-Operative bodies laying on the ground. Jamie initially thought they all died from radiation exposure, but she sees there is blood on the floor and the walls. Jamie thinks that something is more wrong than it currently is as she can tell that these operatives did not die from the nuclear meltdown. She pulls out the Phantom-Maker and turns her communicator back on.

Jamie (worried): Guys, something's not right here. This place is full of body all over.
Peter: Maybe they died from the meltdown and the explosion.
Jamie: That's what I thought too. But, these bodies have bullet wounds and there's blood on the floor and walls. From the looks of these bodies, they were killed with standard Onyx Technology.
Peter: I can bet money that Agent-Thomas is involved with this.

Suspicion grows deep in Tom as he thinks of Agent-Thomas being in Zodiac.

Tom: Hurry and find those jammers, Jamie. I got a feeling Agent Thomas might know what happened. He may actually be involved somehow.

Jamie stops before a massive hole in the floor with the completely dark missile launching station with a body hanging outside of the doorway. The hole leads to the jammers, six floors below the surface. She drops down the floor where the jammers are located and makes a loud landing. Jamie looks forward to see the jammers, lit with dim light, damaged beyond repair with a visible electricity as her detention system on her arm reveals the jammers at top strength.

Jamie: Found the jammer. This thing is completely damaged and the jamming system is out of control.

Peter: Try throwing a frag in it. That should do the trick.

Jamie: Got it.

Jamie takes out an Ultranian frag grenade, lowers the power to only destroy the jammer and not the entire room with her inside, arms it, and pucks the grenade to land inside of the opening in the jammer. The grenade detonates inside, blowing the jammer to pieces and the jamming signal disappears. The force of the explosion was powerful to budge the body near the door to fall down the door.

Jamie: Signal Jammers destroyed.

Peter: Alright, detection signals are clearing up. Captain, I'm marking Agent Thomas's signal for you.

Tom: I'm on my way to it. Jamie, get back to the Omega-Star and Peter, be ready to pick her up.

Peter: Understood.

Jamie: I'm on my way way out of...

Jamie gets caught off-guard when the body near the door falls down right before her. Jamie falls backwards, screaming in fear as the falling body startles her. Jamie is left breathing hard.

Tom: Jamie, report!

Peter: Girl, what the hell is wrong with you?

Jamie gets back on her feet and begins to inspect the body.

Jamie: Sorry guys, a dead body fell right in front of me.

Tom: Let's not waste any more time out here. Hurry up and get out of there, Jamie. I got a visual on Agent Thomas.

Peter: How is he, Captain?

Tom: His Onyx battle-suit is damaged and he's unconscious with faint vitals.

Peter brings up the discussion with Tom of how they do not trust Agent Thomas and what he has done under the command of Former-Generalissimo McAllen.

As Peter brings up this topic, Jamie gets a closer look on the body and sees that it has the "Black Lightning Cross," the symbol of the Thunderbolts unit. Jamie gets a bad feeling with weakened legs and shaking palms as she knows this person is one of them. Jamie flips the body over to its back; she recognizes the armor style and deeply hopes that this body is not who she thinks it is. With her legs weak and her tail shaking, she lifts the body forward in order to press the button on the back of his neck to disassemble his helmet. She looks at the face of the dead Thunderbolt; she recognizes the face and is in horror and pure sadness as she holds the dead body of her teammate and her dear good friend, Tony Vane. His lifeless body is held in Jamie's arms, Jamie's tears cover Tony's lifeless as she realizes that another lifelong friend is dead.

Peter: Jamie, I'm at the Nuclear-Base. What's your status?

Jamie (sobbing): I... I found... I found Tony, guys.

Tom (serious curious): What do you mean you found Tony?

Peter: Yeah, Jamie. His signal is nowhere around here.

Jamie (angry): What do you two think that means?! He's dead, you idiots!

She holds Tony tighter and cries harder. Tom is speechless and Peter gets angry.

Tom: What?!

Peter (infuriated): Sonofabitch! Goddammit!

Tom falls to his knees after hearing that his dear, lifelong friend, who he grew up with in the academy along with Bridgette and Jacob, is dead. He looks at Agent Thomas again and jumps to the conclusion that Agent Thomas is involved and possibly killed him due to his previous history of endangering and even trying to kill his fellow Thunderbolts.

Tom (frustrated): Jamie, get back to the ship and bring Tony's body with you. Peter, hurry up and get here after you pick up Jamie. And hurry up, both of you.

Tom tears through the snow to Agent Thomas, who is unconscious and is leaning on a tree. He sees that Agent Thomas's helmet is cracked and gets the idea to take off his helmet as he stands over them. Nobody, besides Former Generalissimo McAllen, has seen the face of Agent Thomas's helmet. Some of the Thunderbolts, like Peter, Antonio, Jamie, and Jacob, began to think that he has no face inside there and that he was a robot, pretending to be human. Tom sees this as the perfect opportunity and decides to remove his helmet without caring about any other option. Rather than disassembling his helmet, Tom decides to tear off the helmet with little care, just to not break Agent Thomas's neck. Tom tears the helmet off his head and instantly goes into shock as he looks at Agent Thomas's face and his Pink-Eyes.

CHAPTER IX
Lack of Humanity

As Tom's team searches for the other Thunderbolts, Antonio is three miles underneath the surface of the Magnus-Ruins, Terra-Swimming towards the bunker to activate the Underground-Generators. As he goes deeper underground, he begins to think about what happens if the Terrans[53] find him underground. The fact that the Terrans are extremely hostile to Surface-Dwellers and deemed them all kill on sight makes him tunnel faster than he usually does. Antonio wants to go in fast and get out faster because a single Terran is far stronger than he is and he cannot think of a way to take them down without his own Ultranian Battle-Suit. Antonio overthinks the situation to the point where he slams face-first into the outer wall of the bunker.

Antonio: Shit!

Richard: What happened, soldier?

Antonio: I ran into the metal bunker. Goddamnit that hurts…, fuck!

Richard (annoyed): Hurry up and get inside of the bunker.

Antonio: I'm telling you commander, I got a bad feeling about being down here. You know about the Terrans?

Richard: Yes, the creatures with Terra-Powers and are said to be humans who evolved to live underground. What about them?

Antonio: Well, they are civilized. Years back, they were not too happy with surface "Surface-Dwellers" going anywhere near their territory

---

[53] A species of Humans with Terra-Powers who reside underground as Humans reside on the surface and mermaids reside underwater. Average Male 10ft tall; Average female 9 ft. To calculate an average Terran's strength, take every single attribute of the best normal humans and multiple those numbers by 20.

miles underground, me especially. Going down here is like being near a crime scene with warrants. They think I'm an abomination that should be killed on sight. They see me down this deep below ground again, they will fuck me up.

Richard: Well, if this goes as planned, you won't have to encounter the Terrans. According to my E.O.M., some of the generators are already activated.

Antonio: Then shouldn't I be heading back to you? I mean something's practically doing our job for us.

Richard: I want to know who or what's activating these generators and I'm ordering you to go down there. Report back to me when you find out what's causing these generators to reactivate.

Richard cuts communication to make Antonio get to his task.

Antonio: Okay, I have to risk getting my ass handed to me on a platter by Terrans because of some generators underground are being turned on by god knows what. I thought yesterday was shitty.

Antonio uses his Terra-Sense[54] to find the lowest point of the underground bunker and he finds large puncture holes in the bottom of it. He Terra-Swims to the bottom and goes through. He sees dead Onyx soldiers and dead Terrans all across the underground generator chamber the second he makes his way inside. The inside of the bunker has been drenched in the blood of Onyx and Terrans. Antonio cannot detect anymore Onyx soldiers with his holo-map, but he can tell there are more Terrans; he sees that the Onyx were not the ones who killed the Terrans.

Antonio: Commander, we got a huge problem.
Richard: What's happening?
Antonio: It's a mass of dead bodies here.
Richard: Elaborate.

---

[54] A Terra-Deity's ability sense the Earth around him. Antonio will be able to sense whatever is underground and is able to manipulate Earth for about a mile away.

Antonio: Judging from the looks of this, a bunch Terrans beat us here.

He grabs a dead soldier's hands and puts it in the pool of blood near him and sees the blood is still liquified.

Antonio: And the blood is still fresh. It looks like there was a super fierce battle down here.

Antonio hears an explosion.

Antonio: And it sounds like there's a fight still going on.
Richard: What's the status of the generator.
Antonio: It's actually online. But, I doubt the Terrans are the ones bringing these generators online.
Richard: Keep searching then.
Antonio: There may be something else down here. I'm looking at massive-ass claw marks and sword slash marks in the dead Terran bodies.
Richard: Maybe whatever is fighting these Terrans is bringing these generators back online. We need to know what it is.
Antonio: Commander, there is something that you do not understand about me. I am a type of Human called the "Chicken-Shit" when it comes to Terrans and a Chicken-Shit do not investigate murderous Terrans that would slaughters only Surface-Human they see; in fact, we run so we do not end up next. That is a scientific fact.
Richard: I'll take this "fact" under advisement. Now get going. We're short on time.

Richard cuts communications again.

Antonio: Goddamnit. This is not a good look. I have to look for a thing that might have big ass swords and deep as fuck claws strong enough to tear through a damned Terran. I've seen steel machetes, sawed-off shotguns, and chainsaws do nothing to these sonsofbitches or even slow them down and there's something here picking them apart and I have to find out what it is. This is some new-level bullshit.

Antonio has full use of his Terra-Powers and creeps through the hallways, walking past the dead Onyx and Terrans laying on the floor. As he makes his way through the bunker, he encounters a few soldiers and Terrans warriors who were barely alive and struggling to stay alive. The Onyx soldiers die as soon as they startle Antonio and beg for him to help them and/or turn back; the Terrans try to fight Antonio, but drop dead from their wounds via claw marks and sword wounds.

Antonio eventually reaches the second to last generator and sees that it hasn't been activated.

Antonio: Okay, this generator hasn't been activated yet. I don't know if that's a good thing or a bad…

He gets blindsided from being tackled by a Terran that was playing dead. The Terran roars in Antonio's face; Antonio quickly uses a pile rock to form a rock-arm, punches the Terran in the face, and kicks the Terran back. Antonio gets back on his feet, build entire rocky armor, and gets in a fighting stance. He does not see any way out.

Antonio: You ugly ass, ashy-ass, and unreasonably big-ass bitch. You Terrans seriously need toothbrushes.

The Terran roars again, charges, and punches Antonio dead in the chest with enough force to send him flying ten feet away. Antonio lands hard on his back with critical damage to his armor. Antonio is groaning as he gets up slowly, with his entire body aching.

Antonio: <Groan> Shit…! Why is he so buff?!

Antonio gets up on his feet, watches the Terran charge at him to knock his head off; he barely dodges the punch, and counters with a straight jab in the nose. Antonio then delivers a series of blows to the Terran's vulnerable parts, the body parts with flesh exposed, and follows with a drop-kick to send the Terran back. The Terran swings at Antonio; Antonio blocks the punch. He struggles to keep the fist back while the Terran puts in little effort to overpower Antonio. Antonio throws the fist to the left and kicks the Terran in the nose with full force. The Terran looks at Antonio as he whips the blood from his face and cracks its neck. Antonio sees that his attacks didn't even phase this battle-hardened Terran; his attacks only made it angrier. Antonio begins to re-think all of his life-choices while being fearful for his life.

Antonio (fearful): I'm sorry.

When Antonio feels as if things could not get an worse, two more Terran warriors arrive to back-up the one he is fighting. One of the Terrans is holding the last Onyx soldier, who barely alive, by his head. The Terran crush the soldier's head like a blueberry and throws his body to the side. They are slowly walking towards Antonio.

Antonio (nervous): Fuck my life.

He hears the sound of the generator activating and looks over to see the generator activated. Antonio then hears the Terrans roar, redirects his attention to them, and sees one of the Terrans charging at him. Unable to dodge, Antonio instantly puts his arms in front of his face, attempting to block. The Terran raises his fist in order to deliver another blow to Antonio, who expects to feel the force of a speeding truck, he sees a flash of light which lasted for a split second.

After the flash, he sees the Terran not moving. Antonio looks to his right, after seeing through his peripheral vision, and he sees what appears to be a robotic woman. This woman is Cyborg; her entire body, from head to toe, is armored with experimental Ultranian-Alloy which is to be ten times stronger than normal Legion Ultranian battle armor. No organic flesh is exposed as her once fatally damaged body has gone through cyberization with prosthetic arms, legs, and internal organs. She is equipped with high-powered prosthetic claws that can convert to machine pistol barrels and large swords with the same designs sharp enough to cleave through Ultranian metals like a normal sword through wood. Her armor is black and neon blue with the Black Lightning Cross on her back and the upper left part of her chest. The designs of her armor resemble that of a Panther. She stands straight and flicks the blood of her sword. Antonio activates the Onyx-Grade suit he has on and looks at the Cyborg to see his suit's detection systems mark her as an ally, named "Cyborg-Soldier XVII: *Panther*." He redirects his attention to the Terran in front of him and sees a massive amount of blood squirt out of the Terran's neck. The Terran falls out back and chokes on it's own blood. Antonio cannot believe what just happened.

Antonio: What the fuck?!

The other Terrans roar in rage, one Terran charges to Panther and delivers a full-force punch; Panther does not try to dodge the punch, instead she effortlessly blocks it with the palm of her hand. Antonio is dumbstruck as he knows that a full-punch from a Terran is equal to that of the force of a speeding freight train. Panther throws the fist back, activates a lightning field around her from charging her energy, dodges the follow-up punch by jumping on the Terran's arm, activates her Cyber-Claws, Lightning-Dashes[55] through the Terran's head, and lands behind the Terran. Powerful electricity surges out of the Terran's head as he screams in pain before his entire head explodes. As the Terran falls dead, the other remaining Terran, with no ounce of fear, attempts to drop-kick Panther; Panther lightning-dashes, splitting into three different lightning rods around the Terran. The Terran does not see where the lightning rods went, but Antonio sees the rods go behind him, combine to reform Panthers's body. She punches the Terran so hard in the back, her fist goes straight through the Terran's rocky armor and though the Terran's flesh. The Terran goes into shock with Panther's fist inside of his back.

Antonio (cringing): Jesus Christ!

---

[55] When a Lightning-Deity moves rapidly by turning into a rod of Lightning.

Panther, with her fist inside of the Terran, fires beam of lightning out of her hand. The lightning bursts out of the Terran's body and nearly hits Antonio. She pulls her fist out of the Terran's back and pushes the now dead Terran forward so he would not block her view of Antonio. Antonio is scared beyond words as Panther looks at him. Antonio stands still like a dear in headlights.

Antonio (fearful): Shit. Shit. Shit. Shit. Shit. Shit. Shit. Shit. Shit. Shit.

Panther looks at Antonio and she quickly wants to run away from him, not wanting to see her. Antonio thinks that she wants him to follow her; he thinks about how he wants to in a sexual way after seeing that her chest is large (F-Cup to his estimates) and her butt is perfect to him. But he mainly thinks about how he doesn't want to, thinking he will end up like the Terrans if he gets too close to her. Antonio activates his commutator to contact Richard.

Antonio (conflicted): Uh… Commander. I think I found out who's activating these generators. It's a bad robotic female that can easily kill Terrans like they are nothing and has lightning powers.
Richard: "Robotic?"
Antonio: Yes sir, she looks like a robot.
Richard (quietly): The Cyborg-Soldiers Initiative?
Antonio: Uh… I want to say that she's a friend because she has the Thunderbolt symbol on her back. And it looks like she's heading for the last generator But, right now, I'm scared out of my mind.
Richard (urgency): We need more information on this woman. Follow her to the last generator.
Antonio (upset): I was afraid that you'd say that.

Antonio sprints towards the last generator. The battle cries and roars of the Terrans flood the entire bunker as they engage in battle with Panther. He enters the last Generator room to see Panther single-handedly battle ten more Terrans. Panther uses her enhanced maneuverability to strike her foes without being stuck herself. She effortlessly evading the punches and kicks from the Terrans and counters with punches, kicks, and sword slashes with lightning fast speed and clear precision. Panther's attack are strengthened by extreme blind-fury and out-of-control rage.

Antonio: Is it bad to know that my dick is getting hard?
Richard: Focus, soldier.

Panther has taken down two Terrans with slashes of her dual-swords in her counters. She jumps on the shoulders of a Terran, puts her right hand on the Terran's face and her left hand on the back of the his head, and breaks his neck. She jumps off the dead Terran's shoulder over another's head, dodges two punches from two Terrans in the air, but a Terran charges Panther, sending her flying back first into a wall. The force from the impact creates a crater in the wall; she falls on her feet and watches the Terrans roar together with the belief that they are victorious and they begin to close in on her.

Antonio tries to run to her aid, but he stops himself when he sees the designs on her armored-plate turn from neon blue to white; The Terrans notice this change and stop advancing. Panther stands up, charges her energy to unleash more power with an anger-fueled shout, sets her sights on all of the Terrans, and instantly uses her E.C. Focus[56] to lock onto all of the Terrans at once. She charges her swords with her Lightning-Power and Lightning-Dashes in all sides of the Terrans. To Antonio, it appears that a rod of lightning is traveling around the Terrans and nothing is happening. But, what Antonio does not see, Panther is slashing away at all of the Terrans at speed so fast their bodies will not be instantly affected. When she stops seconds after she started, she appears behind the Terrans as they stand completely still; she whips the blood off her swords and places them in the scabbards on her back. When she does this, the Terrans fall apart after lightning surges out of their bodies and turn into large piles of blood, organs, and rocks. Panther's prothetic

---

[56] An E.C. technique that increases the power of an attack with their Energy-Core and allows the user to easily focus their E.C. charged attack with deadly precision. To the user, it appears to them that their sight resembles that of a military targeting-system.

coolant systems pop out of her shoulders, back, and stomach to cool down her systems as increasing her power would cause her systems to heat up. As her systems cool down and colors revert to normal, she calms down as she released a fraction of the anger balled up inside her. However, she still contains a massive amount of anger. Antonio is complete dumbfounded with his jaw dropped as he contemplate the fact he watched a single woman kill thirteen Terrans.

Antonio: Goddamn!

Panther turns her sights on Antonio and Antonio instantly goes silent and still. Antonio thinks to himself that she might attack him and she will easily kill him. She looks at Antonio with fear that he may recognize her and see what the Onyx have transformed her into; she walks backwards in fear of being recognized. Antonio wants to say something to her, but he debating with himself if that is good idea. He thinks of how he can talk to her without possibly setting her off. The best solution that he can think of is to check her out. Antonio looks at a woman's butt when he is too nervous to talk to her in order to boost his confidence ever since he was ten. He looks at Panther's chest, thinking her breast are really big, and her butt is practically perfect to him. However, he throws this strategy out the window after he sees the pile of dead Terran organs. Antonio decides to just simply watch her walk to the generator.

Panther charges electricity her hands, lightning-dashes into the generator's power supply, and grabs it to send the electricity from her hands to the power supply to reactivate the generator. When the generator is fully activated, she sees her reflection on the generator. She puts her hands on her reflection and she gets another glance at what she has become. Her anger rises again; Antonio manages to muster some courage and tries to talk to her but loses it all when she lets out a scream of rage and punches the floor with enough force to crack the metal floor under her. Lightning surges out of her body to resemble her leaking anger.

Panther lightning-dashes into the Generator to escape Antonio and her signal disappears from Antonio's signals. Antonio did not even see her leave; all he saw was a flash. Antonio is completely confused about what just happened. But, he knows that he has to contact Richard to tell him the news about the generator.

Antonio: Commander, this is Antonio. The Generators are reactivated, but the robot-chick got away.
Gordon: I though it was you, little rocky.

Antonio goes silent and becomes fearful just from hearing Gordon's voice.

Gordon: I can remember when you were a little boy who wanted to be part of my gang like your older brother and sister.
Antonio (fearful): Apex-General.
Gordon: I'm glad to know you remember me.
Antonio: How are you contacting me with the Commander's communicator?
Gordon: You lead me to him. When I got here, my soldiers have told me about numerous signs of seismic activity. We tracked it and it lead us to him. And now, I have a far bigger prize than you Thunderbolts. I have the Supreme Commander of the entire Onyx army in the place of the Thunderbolt leader. Try to follow me and he dies, but if you want to extend his time breathing you'll contact Tom Sullivan and every other Thunderbolt he's found to surrender.
Antonio: What's the point of surrendering if you plan to kill him anyway?
Gordon: That doesn't matter to me in the slightest. You kids truly believe that you can make a fool out of me and not suffer the consequences. You Thunderbolts are going to rue the day you choose to stand against the Apex-General. You have five hours to contact them, don't waste it.

Gordon cuts communications.

Antonio: Right when I thought thinks couldn't get any worse. How do I explain this to the Captain?

CHAPTER X
A Second Chance

Half an hour passed after Tom and Jamie found Agent Thomas and Tony's body. Peter is upset with the news of Tony and how Tom and Jamie are placing Agent Thomas and Tony in Preservation-Chambers, which are built to keep injured soldiers into a painless sleep to preserve their physical status status. Peter watches with contempt as they put Agent Thomas inside one of the three chambers while Apex operates the auto-pilot. Kylie is restraining herself from trying to murder Agent-Thomas on the spot. However, the biggest feeling in the ship is bafflement in Tom as he keeps what he discovered a secret from everyone.

Jamie (upset): Captain, remind me why we're taking this son-of-a-bitch with us?

Tom seals the Preservation-Chambers with Agent Thomas and Tony.

Tom: We need every hand we can get right now, Jamie. And I have questions that only he can answer.

Kylie: I say we should kill him.

Beth: Okay, what's all of your beef with this guy?

Tom: A year ago, Agent Thomas nearly got us all killed on numerous occasions. And he was involved in the deaths of hundreds of innocent people.

Beth: Damn… How the hell is he still a Thunderbolt?

Peter: This asshole is from the former Generalissimo before our current leader. He came before Kylie and everyone else. He's permanently assigned to the Thunderbolts and we cannot get rid of him regardless of what he does thanks to the old-ass councilmen. I agree with Jamie and Kylie, we should ditch this punk before he gets us all killed, Captain.

Tom: We can debate this after I find out why he and Tony were in the Zodiac Nuclear Base and after we finish this mission.

Jamie: That'll be a quick debate then. We should just get rid of him right now.

Peter: Yeah, and I got the perfect story to cover it up. "As the base went through its meltdown, Agent Thomas's all Onyx, non-Ultranian, armor was completely shattered in the blast like a museum relic being dropped on the floor. He lost all of his strength, his weaponry was deemed unusable, and by the time we reached his location, we found his Onyx badge in the mouth of a mutated bear," Agreed?

Jamie (disappointed): Really, Peter? Eaten by a mutated bear? Are you serious?

Peter: Hey, I'm just trying come up with ideas here.

Kylie (serious): Try explaining that to the High-Council. They'll find out that you're lying if we went with that stupid story.

Beth (disappointed): Seriously, "A mutated bear?" Man, that's all you got?

Peter: Do you have any better ideas, Beth?

Beth: The way you guys make him out, we should just drop his ass right now, get a box and a shovel, bury him in the dirt, and write, "Gone…. and forgotten."

Peter laughs out loud after picturing himself do that.

Peter (amused): Now that was good. I think you're going to fit in the group just fine.

Beth: I hope so. It's all I have now.

Tom looks out the window and recognizes the general area, despite it used to be a lush green plateau turned gray barren wasteland.

Tom: Okay, all laughs and grievances aside. Peter, how long will take us to reach Jack?

Peter: ETA in five minutes.

Tom: Alright, get ready to move out.

Tom, Peter, and Jamie gear up in case they get into a fight. Tom sees that Jamie is silent with different face on her as she thinks about Jack.

Jamie: Hey, Captain… I think it would be best if I go to find him by myself.

Tom: Are you sure this is a good idea, Jamie?

Jamie: Positive. Why do you ask?

Tom: You and Jack have gotten close. It's possible that your feelings for him might affect your judgement and vice versa.

Jamie: It's not like that, captain. I don't have feelings for Jack, other than him being a friend.

Beth (smirking): Girl, don't give us that. I've heard more times than I can count on two former lovebirds I know. Admit it, you love this guy, don't you?

Kylie: Shut up, Beth.

Peter begins to laugh.

Jamie (blushing): We are just friends… I mean, we're both contain Animal-Spirit Hosts and we know of the Brotherhood and we're on the same side in a war.

Beth: "Brotherhood?"

Jamie: That's a topic for another day. Right now, we need to worry about finding him.

Peter (playfully): Yeah Beth, that's for another day. Right now, we need to find Jamie's boyfriend before we go wherever we're going.

Jamie (blushing): Shut up, Peter!

Beth begins to laugh as she used to see the same thing with Kendall and Kylie.

Peter: Come on, Jamie… we all know you want him. I notice how you
    stare at him when he take his shirt off in the simulation rooms when
    he's training.

Jamie (upset): I'm going to pretend you didn't just said that. Captain,
    I'm certain I can make it to him faster and possibly stealthier if I
    go in alone. Just let me go in alone to find him.

Tom: Alright, Jamie… But if you need backup, just call.

Jamie: Thanks Captain.

The Omega-Star hovers over the remains of Kinto-Park near Jack's
position. Jamie puts the Phantom-Maker on her back, checks her
grappling-hooks, adjusts her Hover-boots, and checks her Super-Sense.
When gearing up, she begins to grow a feeling that Jack needs her. Tom
gives Jamie an Over-Shield.

Tom: You may need this.

Jamie: Thanks, Captain.

Peter: Alright, the tracking-systems are online. You ready, Jamie?

Jamie: I'm good, Peter.

The Cargo-Bay opens over the park; Jamie jumps out of the Omega-
Star; Peter takes control of the Omega-Star and takes off into the skies.

Peter: Try not to have too much fun without us.

Jamie: No promises, Peter.

Jamie grapples to a rooftop and maneuvers through Kinto-Ruin in
higher elevation. She see how the desolate city is completely destroyed
with the surface cracked open, the destroyed buildings, the blackened
skies darker than the night, and a cold and death-ridden wind flowing
through the lifeless streets. However, the average citizen of Kinto, like
Jack and his siblings, would say these ruins are no different from the
environment they grew up in. Jack and his sibling have all spent their
lives in Kinto while it was ran by the Apex-General back when he was
the highest ranking crime-lord before the Legion made him its highest

ranking general. He ruled the city's crime-world with an iron-fist; citizens would cowering in fear by the mention of his name; the police were too afraid to arrest or convict any of his thugs; and he had the politicians under his thumb. Jamie has been in Kinto before and she can recall all of the horrible things Jack has shown her about the city he grew up and tried to raise his siblings in.

Jamie: I hate to say it, but Kinto looks and feels no different. The feeling of death is still in the air. Hope in this city died a long time ago.

As Jamie advances closer to Jack, she gets to street-level and sees the sight of an extremely fierce battle; numerous scorched Legion soldiers and the destroyed remains of Legion vehicles are scattered all over the entire street. Jamie turns on her communications as she moves in to investigate.

Jamie: It looks a fierce battle went through here.
Tom: What did you find?
Jamie: These bodies are still hot, as if they were straight out of an oven or a flamethrower. Jack must've dealt with these goons before he got to his destination. And it looks like this is very recent.
Tom: Do you have any idea where Jack might be?
Jamie: I have one idea.

She continue down the path to Jack through the Kinto-Ruins, still thinking about how Jack may feel about seeing the city that he fought for so long to protect from Gordon be destroyed by him and the army he commands.

Jamie makes her way to the old warehouse that she first met the Turbo-Family. This was where the Turbo-Family would secretly live in as they were all marked kill on sight by Gordon. Jamie recalls Jack telling her how he and his oldest-younger brother, Gibson[57], were left to raise Oz, Antonio, Sparks, and Diane by themselves. They knew that

---

[57] Third oldest in the Turbo family. Telepath. Caucasian. Black Hair. Blue eyes. Someone who simply wanted to help his struggling older brother. Age 20

nobody could help them without getting killed by Gordon's gang, the Apex Syndicate; so Jack and Gibson had to raise their four siblings and the four siblings had to spend their childhoods in hiding with the fear of death lingering over them. When she gets a visual on the warehouse, Jamie puts out her sniper and looks through the scope to get a closer look of the warehouse. She looks through a broken window and turns on the Infrared-Vision of her scope, this would allow her to see an individual's heat-signals. She sees Jack through the Infrared-Vision. Jack's custom-made Thunderbolt battle armor would normally hide his extremely large heat-signal to prevent him from getting detected by infrared scanners, but suit has taken too much damage to mask his signal. Jamie sees that Jack is on his knees as is he is crying as he looks over a body with no heat signal.

Jamie: Captain, Peter, I have a visual on Jack. Group up to these coordinates.
Tom: Understood.
Peter: On my way.

Jamie can tell that something is wrong because the only time she would ever see him cry was when he remembers Maria[58]. She makes her way through the broken window. She can get a clearer visual on Jack and sees that he is under a dim colored light and she can hear his sobs. Jamie and his siblings are the only ones who has ever seen or heard Jack cry and he would rarely cry. She jumps down and lands to see the numerous Legion soldiers that died by Jack's hands. Jamie slowly walks closer to Jack; Jack would normally pay attention to whenever someone is near him, but he is too filled with grief to notice Jamie in the room. When Jamie touch his shoulder to get his attention, Jack turns rapidly, brushes her hand off, grabs Jamie by the neck, and encases his other fist in fire, ready to blow her head off. Startled, Jamie puts her hands up out

[58] Second Oldest in the Turbo Family. Someone who was like a Mother to her suffering siblings, even her older brother. Ivy Deity. Green hair. Green eyes. Shoulder length hair. Deceased. Age 21

of complete reflexes, looking into the flame of anger in his uncovered Inferno-Eye[59].

Jamie: Jack, WAIT! It's okay.

Jamie reaches for the button on the back of her helmet to disassemble her helmet for Jack to see her face, but Jack tightens his grip on her neck as he does not know what she is going to do. Jamie presses the button to disassemble her helmet and show Jack her face.

Jamie: It's me... Jamie.
Jack: Jamie?

He lets go of her neck and dissipate the fire in his fist.

Jack: You're alive.

Before she can even utter a response, Jamie is caught off-guard when Jack suddenly hugs her. Jack believed that he lost everyone he knew: his remaining siblings, Oz, Antonio, Sparks, and Diane, and the closest friend he's ever made, Jamie. Jack lets tears of relief and sadness flow out of his eye, even the bottom of the eyepatch is beginning to get wet from tears from the Lightning-Eye[60]. Jamie can feel the sadness inside of Jack, even through both of the body armor. Jack would fall down to his knees and Jamie was taken to her knees from Jack's body weight. Jack holds her tightly and cause her to blush; Jamie looks over his shoulder to see who his crying over. She see that the dead body in the dim lighting is Jack's oldest-younger brother, Gibson. When she recognizes Gibson, tears begin to come out of Jamie's eyes because she met Gibson and she

---

[59] The Fire-Red eyes that Inferno-Deities possess at Birth. Jack only possesses one Inferno-eye being his right eye because he had acquired the Electric-Blue Lightning eye in his left eye. He cannot use both powers at once. So he can only have one eye open and he has the other covered by an Eye-Patch.

[60] An ability that Jack wields that allows switch his powers from fire to lightning. When his Inferno-Red right eye is open, he is using his fire powers. When his Lightning white left eye is open, he is using his lightning power.

knew how much he meant to Jack. Jamie hugs Jack, now knowing what he is going through.

Jamie (sincere): Oh, Jack… I'm so sorry.
Jack (sobbing): They killed Gibson, Jamie. The Legion found out where he was… I tried to stop them…, but I was too late. Gordon's punishing me, Jamie. Gibson is dead because of me… just like Maria.

Jamie knows where this is going to go.

Jamie: Don't put this on yourself… You need to be strong, Jack. We have to keep fighting.

Jack lets go of Jamie and stands up.

Jack (resentful, growing anger): What's the point now? What's the point of fighting for this hellhole we call Earth? What has this world done for us? It's given us nothing, but pain and misery. Given it to me, given it to you… all of us, especially Gibson, Oz, Antonio, Sparks, and Diane. All I've done was try; I've tried to raise them on my own after Maria was killed; I've tried to keep them from all of this fighting; I'm trying to make sure they all stay alive, but now, all I've done was in vain and they all might be taken away from me, too. Because of the Phoenix… I've been through so much hell because of this spirit. Everything that has happened to me has tied back to this damned bird…, this curse! I actually thought that I can fix this curse when I met Kendall because he had a curse like mine, the curse of the Dragon, but he's gone too. Wherever I go, whatever I do, pain and misery follows me and whoever is close to me will burn because of me…

Jamie slaps him in the face with armor-less hand to make him stop talking; she would've never expected Jack to lose hope after going through the hellish childhood he had and survived with his siblings.

Jamie (angry): Get a hold of yourself…! I know that all of us have been through hard times. Believe me, I've been through so much pain in the circus, being shunned, abandoned, and worse things that I don't even want to talk about. But, there's more to life than pain and misery... You know that. I know that. I learned that while I met all of my friends, Isabel, Tom, Peter, and every other Thunderbolts. Why can't just give up you and Peter get that through your thick skulls?! Life has been cruel to all of us, to every single one of us Thunderbolts. But now it's giving us a second chance with each other. We've all lost people, Jack. But, we can't just give up on our futures because our pasts were tainted... that would be completely unfair to everyone who we've lost, to everyone we have now, and to ourselves!

Jack: What's left, Jamie? What kind of future do we have now? Look around you, Jamie! This world is completely left in ruins. We're pinned against forces this world has never seen before. There's no future for this world! There's no future for any of us, either!

Jamie: There is a future for us! That future is the one where we survive and rebuild everything that the Legion destroyed. But, in order to make that future come to pass, we have to stay together! All of us! And we can't let anything tear us apart!

Jack goes silent, still containing resentment inside of him. Jack is also feeling anger in his conflicting feeling. He does not want to admit to himself; but deep down, he knows that she is right. Peter feels the same as Jack as he stands with Tom in the entrance of the warehouse, after hearing every single word Jamie told Jack. Tom puts his hand on Jamie's shoulder; she looks at his face and sees him smile at her after hearing the truth in her words.

Tom (To Jack): Listen, Jack, hope isn't lost just yet. We are retreating to formulate a plan to continue this fight. But, we need your help to win this war.

Jack: What about...

Tom: Antonio is still in Magnus, fighting in the shadow like you taught him. And Oz, Sparks, and Diane are with Bridgette, evacuated before the city was destroyed. They're safe.... Listen, Jamie was speaking the truth when she said we have a chance to win this fight and a second chance in life for all of us. I know you are upset that you lost your brother, Gibson, but you still have three other brothers and a sister that still need you. I would advice you to not give up here, for their sake and your own.

Jack thinks about how he has to protect his remaining siblings now. Jack takes the small pouch from Gibson's hands, realizes what he has to do now.

Jack: Alright then. I'll fight. But, I don't know for how long.
Tom: That's good enough. Alright, let's move out.

Peter calls the Omega-Star, making it lower down, and open the Cargo-doors. Tom leads Jack into the Omega-Star. Before Jamie gets inside, Peter puts his hand on her shoulder to stop her and get her attention. Her speech truly gave him his motivation back.

Peter (touched): I don't know when you became one hell of a speaker. Thank you.
Jamie: I'll never give up on this fight. Because I want to see our futures together, for all of our sakes and everyone we lost. I just hope you won't give up either.

Jamie looks at Peter to see that he is still sad over Isabel and turns around to give him raise her fist for a fist dap; Peter gives Jamie a fist dap in memory of Isabel Stratton. They step inside of the Omega-Star. When Jamie sits right next to Jack, sees that Jack is still upset, and put her hand on Jack's hand to comfort him. Jack feels Jamie's hand on his; they smile at each other; Jack turns his hand to hold Jamie's hand.

Peter: Alright, time we finish this fight. Next stop, Magnus.

The Omega-Star rapidly leaves the skies of the Kinto-Ruins, launching to its next and possibly final destination: the Magnus-Ruins.

CHAPTER XI
Do-or-Die

A hour passes after the group found Jack and Antonio has spent three of the five hours Gordon gave him to try to use the E.O.M to contact Tom and the other Thunderbolts. After numerous attempts to contact them, he finally manages to contact them after nearly breaking it several times. He had to break the news to Tom about Richard and Tom is not happy about it.

Tom (outraged): What do you mean, "Apex-General took the Commander?"

Antonio: I mean they took him. They detected the seismic activity my Terra-Powers create and they tracked my movements underground to where I left him. He wants all of us to surrender or else he'll just kill the commander.

Tom (irritated): Unbelievable… This damned old-man must've known we would go to Magnus so he waited for us there.

Antonio: Captain, he also said if he thinks we're up to something, he'll kill the commander. He'll expect to see you, Captain, along with me, Jamie, Peter, and especially Jack. I got a feeling that if he doesn't get us all, he'll kill the commander. We need a good plan here.

Tom begins to remember a hypothetical scenario that he and Richard planned in case Richard was captured by enemies and Tom was the only one to fight.

Tom: Is he still in an Ultranian Warship?

Antonio: Yeah, his signature warship. It's been floating over Magnus for the past three hours.

Tom: Does the E.O.M say, "Initiate Operation: Marathon" on the top of the screen.

Antonio looks at top of the screen and it says Initiate Operation: Marathon on the top.

Antonio: How do you...?
Tom: That's all I need to hear.

Tom used his Bridgette's communications station to project Bridgette and Antonio's face on the monitor. All of the Thunderbolts are in the Cargo-Bay, even Peter with Apex guiding the autopilot to fly outside of Gordon's detection range.

Tom: Alright, Thunderbolts, this is it. As you all know, Peter, Jamie, and I escaped Mundi-Castle to find everyone of you for this evacuation plan customized by the Commander. But, before we go anywhere, we need to rescue Commander Sullivan from the Gordon.
Jamie: Do you have a plan, Captain.
Tom: I do, but if it's going to work, then it's going to require a massive amount of teamwork, something that I know we have.
Peter: Just lay it on us, Captain.
Tom: It's actually quite simple. For a start, we're going to have to split into teams of two; Jamie, Peter, Jack, Antonio, and I will be Team-A and Kylie, Beth, and Bridgette will be Team-B. Team-B, you'll be back in Magnus, Bridgette will mark these points in each of these city districts and she'll tell you how to activate the dormant city guns underground.
Kylie: City Guns?
Tom: When Magnus was developed during the Shadow-Wars, the Onyx built hidden skyscraper-sized defense guns that will activate in case the city gets destroyed and when the Exodus Protocol gets activated. That's one of the things that the Underground Generator system under the city powers up. These Cannons should have the power to do damage to Gordon's armada.

Peter: Gordon has to have eyes on the ground. How can have any team activate these guns.

Tom: That's where Team-A comes in. We're going to get Gordon to drop his guard as we surrender.

Peter: Huh?

Jamie: Wait, what?! Surrender?!

Peter: Captain, we just escape the slammer earlier today and we're on the lamb. How can we just turn ourselves in?

Tom: In order to save our friends, we need to conduct a forgotten Onyx strategy called, "Trojan-Tactics." We're not really turning ourselves in; we're going to make it look that way. He needs us alive for the Dark-Knighten and he does not know about everyone else. If we go in, we will have Gordon lower his guard for everyone else to operate without suspicion.

Peter: This sound a tad too risky; even for us Captain.

Tom: It's a risk we'll have to take. It'll be easier than we think; Gordon is going through Victory Disease, he's getting overconfident from the series of victories he has over all of the Onyx Generals, especially when he captured me and Jamie via ambush. He'll go down like Napoleon and George Armstrong Custer. He already compares himself to Julius Caesar.

Antonio: How do we escape?

Tom: Peter will have Apex activate the Omega-Star's flares to blind everyone there and we'll back to the Omega-Star and we lead them to deal with the City-Guns.

Bridgette: Those guns can deal damage to the fighter-jets, but they aren't built to take on a Ultranian Warship.

Tom: No but, it'll slow them down for the commander to commence this evacuation. All we need to do is to be within the city-limits.

Antonio: This plan sounds crazy, Captain.

Jack: It may be crazy, but, we're doing it.

Kylie: How will we be evacuated?

Tom: I don't know that much. Maybe Bridgette can tell us.

Bridgette: All I can say Oz, Sparks, Diane, Zack, and I are off-world.

Antonio: "Off-World?" What, like another planet?

Bridgette: Pretty much, yeah.

Tom: Alright, we got our plan. Peter, take us down to Shinto-Plaza.
    Antonio, meet us there.

Peter: Got it.

Antonio: Yes sir.

Tom: Everyone else, gear up. We may be in for a fight.

The Omega-Star lands in Shinto-Park, where Antonio is waiting for them with the E.O.M in his hands. Inside, everybody gears up for the final fight. Each of them takes their Battle-Suit converters from the repair chamber of the ship and equip them to their persons; Tom places his on his waist in its belt form; Jamie places hers on her diaphragm and activates its shoulder belt form; Peter puts on his Mark II backpack and gives everyone Signal-Jammer accessories for their suits to shield their signals; Kylie puts on her converter gauntlet; Jack places his newly repaired converter on his left arm into its arm band mode to hide his mark of the Brotherhood.

As Jack adjusts his eye-patch over his left eye, he thinks about how to tell Antonio, Oz, Sparks, and Diane about Gibson. Jamie sees the worry on Jack's face and she wonders if she should talk to her.

Everyone activates their battle-suits' battle modes and takes out their weapons. Kylie and Beth jump out of the Omega-Star; Peter gives Beth an Ultranian-grade visor for her to see the coordinates of the guns. She pits the visor on her face and all it covers is her eyes.

Beth: Stylish… in the 60s.

Peter: It's these or nothing. Your pick.

Beth: Fine.

Tom: Let's get going.

As the mission commences, the Thunderbolts begin to grow uncertainty if this may be their last fight, a feeling that that they do not usually get because of their past confidence. In the past, they would complete every single one of their missions back when it was only eight of them with no feeling of fear; but as the war rages on and their number begin to decline, they grew a feeling that every soldier has, whether-or-not if this fight will be their last.

Bridgette has marked the location of the four terminals, one in each city district. Kylie and Beth know that they'll get this job done faster if they split up, Kylie would take Shinto and Olympus and Beth takes Aurora and Jacinto. Kylie has an easier time going through city district after being in Magnus before it was destroyed; Beth, on the other hand, has never been in the city and only has the visor to guide her. Bridgette tells them both that they can use their EC-Energy to bypass the passwords and to activate the guns; and this is what they do when they find the terminals for the City-Guns.

Meanwhile with Gordon, he is accompanied by one of the Legion's lower-class Elites as a body guard. Gordon is in the commander's seat of the warship as he gets an incoming transmission. He orders his pilots to put it through and to Gordon's surprise, Dark-Knighten, in an unknown location, is the one who contacts Gordon. Gordon and the Elite bow in respect for Dark-Knighten; Dark-Knighten grows suspicious after seeing Gordon's being the cockpit of his warship.

Gordon (nervousness): D-D-D-Dark-Knighten.

Elite: Big boss man.

Dark-Knighten: What's going on, Gordon?

Gordon: What do you mean?

Dark-Knighten: I can recognize the cockpit of your warship. Now, I'm going to ask again... What's going on, Gordon

Gordon: Uh... there were some slight complications, Dark-Knighten.

Dark-Knighten: What do you mean, "complications?"

Elite: The Thunderbolts escaped Mundi-Castle.

Dark-Knighten (shocked): What?!

Gordon (quietly): I will kill you when this is over.

Elite: Hey, the Dark-Knighten asked a question and it's best to give the man a truthful answer. They even destroyed Omegatronus before they left too.

Dark-Knighten (mixed emotions): You let the Thunderbolts escape...? <Chuckles> You've fucking with me, right? I'm gone for a day and the Thunderbolts escape on your watch? You had one job and you fucked that up!

Gordon: I do have a back-up plan, Dark-Knighten.

Gordon shows Dark-Knighten that he has Richard tied up, blindfolded, and gagged.

Gordon: Dark-Knighten, I present to you... Onyx Generalissimo Richard Sullivan. The supreme leader of the Onyx. I found him under the remains of the Onyx capital city, Magnus. I intend to use him to bring the other Sullivan and his hopeless followers to surrender.

Dark-Knighten (not impressed): <Sigh of irritation> Gordon, that type of plan has been used to death. They'll know it's a trap and they'll find a way around with their eyes closed. It's too predictable!

Gordon: But, they will have no choice but to spring this trap. This is the type of plan that allowed me to capture Sullivan and the Monkey-Girl in the first place. My soldiers ambushed, overpowered, and we brought them back to you.

Dark-Knighten (irritated): The fact that you're still basking in that moment is what worries me. You're letting these victories get to your head!

Gordon: I am not letting my victories get to my head, Dark-Knighten. I am certain this will work. These are inexperienced children and they do not have near as much combat experience as I do. I am the Apex-General and I am certain that my military genius will be more than enough to triumph the Thunderbolts.

Dark-Knighten (irritated): For your sake, it better be more than enough. Do not fuck this up too, Gordon.

Gordon: You won't have to worry about that, Apex-General out.

Gordon stares at the screen with disdain for Dark-Knighten. Gordon has long believed that he is not worthy of being leader of an army the size of the Legion, a feeling that he has had from the beginning, ever since Omegatronus found Dark-Knighten. Gordon thinks to himself.

Gordon (disdainfully): First, you would dare to take the title that I so deserve. Now you are questioning my ability to lead. You're no older than they are, no more experienced than they are, and I am taking orders from you. This shall not go on for long. Thunderbolts or no Thunderbolts, I plan to have reformation in leadership of this army. The Apex-General shall stand over all, where he rightfully deserves to stand.

Gordon looks at the Elite.

Gordon: I hope you know that regardless if we capture the Thunderbolts or not, I will kill you.

Tom, while on Bridgette's station, hacks into Gordon's communications as Jamie, Peter, Jack, and Antonio are getting ready for the Trojan-Tactic plan. He uses the Communications-Station to communicate with Gordon.

Tom (to Gordon): Apex-General, this is Thunderbolt Captain Tom Sullivan. Do you read me? I repeat, Apex-General, this is Thunderbolt Captain Tom Sullivan. Do you read me?
Gordon: How the hell did you get into my communications?
Tom: That's irrelevant. I am contacting you to surrender.
Gordon (shocked): "Surrender?"
Tom: Affirmative.
Gordon: Wait a minute. Didn't you say that an Onyx never surrenders back in Mundi Castle? You even let three soldiers and three civilians, one being a pregnant woman, die because of it.
Tom: Do you not see what is around all of us? Look at what this war has turned our planet. It used to be a planet of prosperity, hope, and life. Now, it's a barren rock with death in the air; billions have died; and societies, cultures, and generations are lost. What is the point of continuing to fight a losing war? Peter Orion, Jamie Kelly, Jack Turbo, Antonio Turbo and I chose this and we are approaching

your position to surrender and turn ourselves in, but under one
condition.

Gordon: I want to hear Jack's voice and have him tell me that.

Jack: It's me, Apex-General. I'm here to surrender too.

Gordon: What about the two in from Denver?

Tom: They had given up in Denver after what you told them and we
had to leave them. Who knows what they're up to now.

Gordon thinks about the situation and sees that he not only has the
Thunderbolts that he is after, but he also has Jack, someone who's been
a splinter in his side for years before the Ultranian Invasion.

Gordon: Very well then..., Tom Sullivan, Jack Turbo. I am glad that
you realize who is the greater power in this world. I am awaiting
your arrival.

Tom: Yes, Apex-General, we will be there shortly.

Tom cuts communications with Gordon. Peter and Antonio can't
believe Gordon believed them.

Peter: Man, for a highly revered military commander who has fought
wars ever since World War II, he is one old fool.

Tom: He's growing overwhelming arrogance. I saw that back in
Mundi-Castle.

Tom (to Antonio): Antonio, you can use the E.O.M, right? What's the
status on the charge?

Antonio: It's at 80% power, the estimated charge time is five minutes.

Tom: Alright, everybody ready?

Jamie: I'm ready.

Peter: I'm always ready.

Jack: Ready.

Antonio: Ready... I guess.

Tom: Peter, have that flare ready.

Peter: Ready and waiting.

The Omega-Star flies to Gordon's personal warship, where Gordon and numerous Legion soldiers stand on the launching platform of the ship. Gordon has Richard blindfolded, tied up, gagged, and a bomb on his neck to prevent any resistance. Gordon looks at the Omega-Star with the airflow blowing in his face, even blowing his hat away and Gordon's eyes are halfway closed with the airflow in his face. The Omega-Star lands and its cargo bay opens. The sound of guns being drawn flows in the air as Tom, Peter, Jamie, Jack, and Antonio walk out of the Omega-Star with their suits in stealth mode.

Peter (to all soldiers): This is all a bit much, even for us.
Gordon: You sound afraid, Thunderbolt. You should rejoice… There are few that have been held prisoner by the Apex-General and is allowed to live to tell about, even for a short while.
Tom: Yes, Apex-General.

They make their way towards Gordon and Richard, who is completely unaware of what they are doing. They notice that Gordon has overwhelming confidence in him, thinking that his military genius has triumphed the mighty Thunderbolt commander, Tom Sullivan twice. To Tom, this is the best possible outcome because he know that overconfidence can taint even the best military commander; he sees that Gordon has Victory-Disease, Napoleon Bonaparte and the Battle of Taierzhuang are prime examples. None of the Thunderbolts were able to take Tom's word for it, but after seeing with their own eyes, they know that Tom is right.

Gordon (overflowing confidence): Now then, prisoners of the Apex-General, if they wish to preserve their lives, bow before him.
Jamie: Can I ask you something, first?
Gordon: What might that be?
Jamie: Why are you speaking in third-person?
Peter: Yeah… I was about to ask that. That sound so weird.

Gordon laughs as he takes the blindfold out of Richard.

Gordon: For you to know the name of the military leader greater than even the Romans. Now then, on your knees.

Tom conceals his amusement over how things are turning out and thinks to himself.

Tom: This is going better than I imagined.

The Thunderbolts, without even communicating, get on their knees slowly in unison. They then slowly moves their hands behind their hands behind their heads. They have their heads in the ground with their hands on the back of their heads. As they lay on the ground, Gordon wants to savor the moment while Richard actually thinks Tom is surrendering for him. Tom, in a split second, gives Richard an Over-Shield.

Tom: Peter, NOW!
Peter: Apex!

The Omega-Star's exterior brightens and it unleashes an extremely bright flash of light that temporarily blinds all of the soldiers, the Elite, and Gordon.

Tom: Take them out, Peter!

To add additional fire power, Peter launches a Death-Disk[61] out of a panel in the back of his shoulder; it charges as it locks on to all Legion signals takes out their fire-arms and opens fire on the Legion surrounding them. An barrage of repulser fire swarms into the soldiers as they drop like flies; the Elite used himself as a shield to protect Gordon. Jack goes to Richard to untie him and remove the gag. Gordon takes out the detonator for neck bomb and detonates it. The bomb explodes

---

[61] A hovering-disk weapon Peter developed to fire out of his armor to hover in the air before firing high-damage repulser fire in all direction below with a targeting system to. But, comes at medium to high cost to his suit's power supply.

on Richard's neck, but it only destroys the Over-Shield on Richard without harming him. Jack fires a fireball at Gordon and the Elite and blow them back. The Thunderbolts make their way to the Omega-Star before Gordon and the heavily damaged Elite, with damage through his armor. They rush to the Omega-Star with Richard; Peter jumps into the cockpit while everyone else is in the cargo-bay. Gordon throws a healing-orb on the Elite to pursue them. The Elite tries to stop them; Jack intercepts the Elite with a powerful elbow to his exposed solar-plexus and kicks the Elite in the chest with his foot incased with fire to blow him back to Gordon. Jack goes in the Omega-Star. Peter jumps into the Cockpit.

Tom: Peter, we can't waste anymore time. Get us out of here!

The Omega-Star takes off from the warship. The Elite gets up and focuses energy in his hand as he locks his sights on the Omega-Star's engine. He fires a high-powered ball of energy and it hits the Omega-Star's engines. The force of the impact makes everyone inside jump all over the place. The Omega-Star's engines are blown and it plummets down to the ground; all Peter can do is a controlled crash. He guides the Omega-Star to Shinto-Plaza, where it plows into the ground before sliding a few meters. Kylie and Beth saw the Omega-Star crash and they rush to Shinto-Park. But, to their surprise, a fleet of Legion fighter jets and drop-ships swarmed out of the warship like a angry bee colony.

The Omega-Star is in extremely poor condition, rendered unable to fly. Even the Cargo-Bay doors are jammed shut with damage to Agent Thomas and Tony's Preservation-Chambers. Jack fires a fireball to blast the cargo-bay doors open and everyone, but Peter, walks out the Omega-Star aching and out of breath. Peter touches the hatch and it falls off. Kylie and Beth approach them all.

Kylie: Is everybody alright?
Peter (extremely sad): No!!! Look at my baby! She's not alright! Goddammit!

Peter begins to actually cry for the Omega-Star, the ship he built with his own two hands. This ship was as precious to him as his suits.

Antonio: Really, Peter? You're going to cry like a bitch over a plane?
Peter: Shut your ashy ass up. You don't know how long I've spent working on this ship.
Antonio: That's just hurtful, man.
Jamie: I'd hate to interrupt your little fight, I really do…, but we got more Legion coming in.

All the Thunderbolts looks up to see swarming the skies. They also see the City-Guns activate and slowly rise up with the ground shaking under them. The Guns open fire on the fleet and cause them to scatter. The Thunderbolts know this will by them time and keep numerous Legion soldiers off of them. Antonio gives Richard the E.O.M. and Richard checks the timers on it and activates a communications hub for all of the Thunderbolts as they all within it's general range.

Richard: Alright, Thunderbolts, we have three minutes until the Teleporter is activated. We just have to hold them off until then.

The Thunderbolts activate the battle-modes, take out their weapons, and gets ready for battle.

Tom: Alright, everyone. There's too many of them to for us to stay bunched up together! Split up and stay within the city limits.
Peter: Oh, I'm ready to kick some ass.

Everyone of the Thunderbolts split in every single direction; Peter would go to the skies and Antonio goes underground. Jack, Tom, and Richard are the only one who did not split up as they watch the Legion ships overwhelm the guns. The Thunderbolts would go their way to fight the Legion armies in their last stand on Earth, utilizing their special abilities, talents, and weapons to survive the attack. The Elite touches down in front of the three.

Jack: Captain, Commander. You two need to get out of here. I'll handle this guy.

Tom and Richard make their way for cover; Tom escorts Richard to safety with the E.O.M.. Jack turns his attention to the Elite.

Jack: If you want to get to them, you'll have to go through me.
Elite: That's fine with me, Jack Turbo: Phoenix of the Brotherhood.

The Elite, allowing his energy to flow in every fiber of his body, dashes straight to Jack and throws a punch; Jack throws a punch of his own with fire flowing through his fist, Fire-fist. Their fists collide; the collision causes a crater in the ground. Jack sees the hatred the Elite's eyes and he can tell from that comment that this Elite Fighter used to be part of the Brotherhood. Their fists separate; the Elite tries to swing-kick Jack in the neck; Jack blocks the kick with his arm, grabs the Elite's leg, pulls it in, and punches the Elite in the face with enough force to send him flying back. The Elite recovers and sees Jack dash towards him; Jack lands lightning-fast fire-powered punches and kicks on the Elite that is even wearing down the Elite's remaining armor. To finish, Jack jumps in the air and dropkicks the elite in the chest with his feet covered in fire-energy to have the kick explode the moment his feet made contact the Elite's chest. Jack lands on his feet and the Elite flies back, backflips off the ground to recover, and slide on the ground with his feet. Jack, not expecting the Elite to go down that easily, steels himself for whatever the Elite tries next. The Elite stand up straight, rubs the blood off his nose.

Elite: I expected no less from the Brotherhood's Phoenix. But, I don't waste time with traitorous trash like you. So let's say that that concludes our warm-up.

Jack disassembles his helmet.

Jack: I'm guessing how you know that name, you must be from the B.O.G.

Elite: That's right. And you betrayed us. Punishment for treason is death!

Jack and the Elite clash and exchange punches and kicks. The Elite kicks Jack in the stomach, causing Jack to stagger from the pain; the Elite charges an energy ball and believes it's enough to kill Jack. Jack quickly recovers and lands a powerful knee the Elite's stomach, dealing major damage, causing the energy ball to dissipate in the Elite's hand and saliva to rush out his mouth. Jack then elbows the Elite in the face with enough force to send him down to the ground and the Elite could not recover fast enough stop himself from feeling the full force of the impact. Jack then charges a high-powered fire-ball and fires it to the Elite and it explodes on impact, dealing major damage on the Elite.

Gordon sees Jack standing over the Elite, ready to deliver the final blow. Seeing no other option, he fires a Omni-Boost Serum[62] from his revolver in the Elite's right butt-cheek and the Elite can feel the sudden increase in power. He instantly glows red and he realizes what has happened to him. The Elite dashes off the ground to Jack and punches in the stomach; Jack takes massive damage and coughs up spit. The Elite then punches Jack in the face with enough force to send Jack flying through buildings.

Elite: YES! I can feel the power!

The Elite flies after Jack. Gordon loads another Omni-Boost Serum into his revolver.

Gordon: Never hurts to have a backup plan.

---

[62] An enhancement serum, created by Dr. Evans, to increase the speed, agility, strength, reflexes, and durability of the user by five times the user's original attributes. The effects are temporary.

Gordon calls in a fighter-jet to pick him up. When a fighter-jet arrives, he climbs inside and orders the pilot to follow the Elite. The fighter-jet pursues Jack and the Elite.

Gordon: All units, these Thunderbolts want a fight. Give them a fight they won't live to regret! Leave none alive! That's a direct order from the Apex-General!

The Omni-Boost has given the Elite enough power to tip the scale in his favor against Jack. The Elite is able to counter Jack blow for blow, outmaneuver Jack, and land critical blows on Jack; and Jack can do little to block or dodge these attacks. The Elite kicks Jack and sends him flying through more buildings. Jamie, fighting other soldiers, has the Elite in her sights and fires a shot from the Phantom-Maker's sniper at the Elite neck; the shot hits the Elite with a direct hit. The Elite is in agony with a repulser bullet going through his neck and sees Jamie take a shoot at him. He holds his neck in pain.

Elite: You Bitch!

The instant the Elite is about to charge at her, he is instantly blasted with a bolt of lightning from Jack. The Lightning is dealing major damage to the Omni-Boosted Elite, completely paralyzing him. When he looks at where the Lightning coming from, he sees Jack, using the Lightning-Eye, lunging at him. Jack kicks the Elite in the jaw, causing the Elite to spin backwards. Jack then stands in front of the Elite, channels lightning in his hands, and grabs the Elite by the arm to send thousands of volts through the Elite's body. The Electricity flowing through the Elite is too much for him as he screams in the air in pain. Jack finishes this by sending the Elite back with a shockwave. Jack follows the Elite.

Tom: Just a little longer everyone, only two minutes.
Peter: I can do this all day, Captain.

Meanwhile with Jack and the Elite, they continue to exchange blows with each other. Jack resorts to switch powers back and forth in order to keep up with the Omni-Boosted Elite. Jack is struggling to block and counter all of his attacks while the Elite's Omni-Boost is beginning to wear off. Their exchanges end when they both punch each other in the cheeks. They both jump back and create a large gap of space between them. They are both out of breath as the Omni-Boost wears off of the Elite. The two of them finds themselves in an alley leading to an old hangout for Onyx cadets. Jack begins to think about how this particular Elite is from the Brotherhood of Gods and begins to grow disappointed in the direction this fight lead to.

Jack: I never thought that I would see the day that a proud member Brotherhood, like you, would go so low as need the help of a Normal[63] to get more powerful. Especially a Normal that was out to destroy the Brotherhood decades ago.

Elite (exhausted): This isn't the first time in the history of our brotherhood that we have had to team up with Normals. I'm sure you of all people should know about the destruction of the corrupted Exodus Island.

Jack: The aftermath of the power-mad lust for blood that consumed the B.O.G.. We were supposed to be above the primitive ways of the "Normals." We were supposed to be gods, higher being due to our amazing gifts. But, it turns out that all of that was simply a lie; we're all mortals like the rest after all, powers or no powers.

Elite (outraged): You dare to compare us gods to these Normal scumbags. We have the power to destroy entire planets, the most powerful among us were able to destroy stars. You and I can easily destroy this rock we can earth. The Normals knew this and they fear us because of it. They have oppressed the likes of us for centuries. Our ancestors have chosen to rise up against their oppression and resist.

---

[63] The name members of the Brotherhood gave to the population who do not have powers.

It made it so blasphemers like you would insult your brotherhood like this.

Jack: It stopped being my brotherhood when they manipulated me, took over my mind, and made me kill innocent people out of their own grudges against their enemies.

Elite: Blasphemer! What did the brotherhood mean to you?!

The Elite is in a state of fury as he gets another Omni-boost from Gordon, who is in the fighter-jet observing the two.

Jack: It used to be liberating life. But now…. the Brotherhood of Gods is dead to me.

Jack sees that he is out of options; he realizes that if he want to win this fight and survive, he will have to use a relic from the distant past that Gibson made him to unlock his hidden powers. He sticks his left hand over a panel in his armor to take out a Super-Pill[64] as it launches to the palm of his hand.

Elite: What's that?

Jack: Take your best guess.

The Elite, knowing his history of the Brotherhood, knows exactly what the Super-Pill is and what kind of power boost it can give Jack. He tries to stop Jack from eating the pill, but Jack quickly conjures a solar-ball, slams it into the ground to blind the Elite and propel himself in the air. Gordon orders the jet's pilot to open fire on Jack; Jack puts the pill under his tongue, fires a fire-wave at the Fighter-Jet, and hits it in one of its engines. The Fighter-Jet crashes down the streets with Gordon inside it. Jack proceeds to eat the Super-Pill. When he swallows the it, Jack

---

[64] A Red-Colored Pill, created by the Brotherhood during the Exodus-Renaissance inspired by the Legendary Super-Knighten, that contain a small sliver of the Power-Enhancing Energy. This pill gives its user a 25x increase in Power, Speed, Agility, Durability, Strength, and Reflexes. Effect vary depending on power and are temporary.

feels nothing for about five seconds and then he instantly feels tense in ever single part of his body from head-to-toe. The Tenseness is the sign of a massive power-surge. Not only can he feel a surge of power, but he can also feel all of the muscles in his body getting tense as they slightly increase in mass. A golden metal headband appears on his forehead over his hairline with the symbol of the B.O.G. as his actual hair turns into fire. Jack feels the surge of power reaching its peak as both of his eyes turn Molten-Orange; his eye-patch burns disintegrates. He unleashes a power-fueled scream as the transformation finishes.

The Elite regains his vision and he sees that he is too late in stopping Jack from using the Super-Pill. They both see that not only has Jack's power drastically increase, but his body has changed. Jack can feel that his muscles are slightly bigger than they originally were and he notices that he can see through both of his eyes at the same time, something that he could not do for years ever since he steal the Lightning-Eye years ago. The Elite can notice that his hair has turned into fire with golden metal headband on his forehead around the flames with the symbol of the Brotherhood on the center of it. Jack is amazed with the feeling of power he has now, despite it being a feeling he never wanted to feel again, but the sensation of seeing through both eyes overwhelms him. The raw power surging through Jack is pushing away all of the ash and dust around him.

Jack (amazed): I… I can see through both of my eyes again.

Jack disassemble the armor on his hands to see his hand and feet in order to use his new strength to the fullest. A tear runs down his face as he realizes this is one of the last things that Gibson made for Jack.

Jack (regret): Gibson, I can control the power surges now. You were right the whole time.

Jack redirects his attention to the Elite, causing the Elite to begin to shake in hidden fear. Jack descends back to the ground to face the Elite. He can see the fear on the Elite's face.

Jack: I'm sure you know what happens when a Deity, like me, takes a Super-Pill. They unlock a power that has never been seen in this era. I've been a cut above the other members of Kinto-Brotherhood while I was a pound member. But now..., I have the power of an true Inferno[65].

Elite: Big deal, your hair is on fire now. That still doesn't mean that you can beat me.

The Elite lunges towards Jack to land a devastating punch into his solar-plexus; Jack did not even try to dodge it. The Elite aims an Omni-Boost powered punch into Jack's solar-plexus, but goes into awe when he realizes that Jack caught his fist with ease.

Jack (amazed): Come on... Is that the best you can do?

The Elite jumps backwards and blasts Jack in the chest, thinking that this would affect Jack, but it does not even phase Jack. Jack begins to walk towards the Elite as the Elite begins to fire a barrage of energy blasts directly at Jack. This would create a large pile of smoke around Jack that he would blow away with a small energy pulse. When the smoke gets pushed away, the Elite sees that Jack is not even phased; his armor doesn't even a single scratch from those blasts as Jack's aura is protecting his armor like shields. Jack then races towards the Elite and lands a powerful blow to his Solar-Plexus, causing the Elite to spit a large amount of blood. Jack follows with an left hook to the jaw with enough force to break the Elite's jaw, another punch in the solar-plexus, knees the Elite in the face, and a right hook to the jaw that sends the Elite flying towards the end of the alley. The Elite slowly recovers and charges towards Jack and tries to land a swing-kick on Jack's neck; Jack blocks with the kick with his arm sending enough to fracture the Elite's left leg

---

[65] The name of the most powerful fire-deities. Beings that create flames that can burn anything in the entire universe. Legend has it, the most powerful infernos in the history of humanity was so powerful, he created a star by igniting hydrogen atoms in his hands. Also said the most powerful Inferno can also destroy stars as big as Betelgeuse.

bones. He then trips the Elite's right leg with a spin kick, grabs the back of the Elite's head, and slams him in the pavement with enough force to create a deep crater. The Elite, as Jack stands over him, asks himself how is Jack overpowering him while he is Omni-Boosted. Jack then opens his right hand, sticks it over the Elite's body as the Omni-Boost wears off, and charges a medium-sized fireball with little to no time at all.

Jack: Burn… with the rest of the Brotherhood!

Jack fires the fireball and on impact, a large surge of fire erupts upward towards the sky. This surge of fire contains more than enough power to disintegrate the Elite body. The Elite screams in agony as he disintegrates before Jack's very eyes. When the fire burns out, the Elite has been turned into ashes and these ashes were blown away by the wind created by Jack's energy, along with all of the other ashes in the air. Jack regrets the fact that he had to relive the vile memories he had as a member of the Brotherhood-of-Gods and he can sense that he is beginning to fall prey to power-lust again. He hears on his communicator that they have one minute left. But, with the warship releasing more and more soldiers and ships onto the city-ruins. He launches in the air and hovers in the air to see everyone fight off the Legion soldiers and Fighter-Jets across the city-ruins. He charges a massive amount of fire-energy in his hand and focuses on the warship. He fires a massive wave of fire with large fire balls spiraling around the wave and has it go full throttle towards the Warship.

While in the air, Peter is eliminating Legion aerial forces as if he was playing an easy gun with the Mark II's stronger systems.

Peter: Bring me another.

Apex then detects Jack's Spiral-Wave and alerts Peter of it. Peter turns his sights to the spiral-wave and watches as it goes straight through the warship's engines, causing it to have system failure and crash with small explosions on it.

Peter: Holy shit!

Jack: Enemy warship destroyed.

Jamie (dumbstruck): Jack, how did you do that?

Peter: That's what I'm wanting to know. Those ships can survive a collision with a asteroid.

Jack: I'll explain later. I have some unfinished business to tend to.

Tom: Alright, let's mop up the rest. We're almost out of this mess.

Richard: Attention all Thunderbolts. The Teleporter shall lock on to all of your signals in fifteen.

As Richard counts down from fifteen, the Thunderbolts are still fighting against the Legion Soldiers on the ground and Jack soars to where Gordon crashed and lands in front of Gordon as he crawls out of the rubble of the crashed fighter jet. Jack looks down at Gordon with complete anger in his eyes and full intent to kill. Gordon looks up to see the hatred in Jack's eyes and sees that there is no way for him to escape.

Gordon: Well… I guess this is the part where you kill me.

By the time he charges his fireball halfway, Richard reaches One and activates the teleporter. Richard glows blue and teleports. Tom and Jamie are opening fire on the Legion soldiers and see that they are beginning to glow blue and they teleport. Antonio sees Tom and Jamie vanish and he is left speechless as he glows blue as well and he teleports.

Apex: Peter, I'm detecting a massive surge of Quantum energy in all of the Thunderbolt. They're being teleported away.

Peter sees that he is glowing blue. He looks to himself for a split second, making him drop his guard down, gets hit by a missile, gets sent to the Omega-Star and both Peter and the Omega-Star teleport.

Beth (to Kylie): Uh, Kylie. Something's happening.

Kylie sees that she is glowing and she activates her Velocity-Boots to rush to Beth. She puts her hand on Beth's shoulder to make her glow blue and they teleport.

Jack get ready to kill Gordon with a high-powered fireball and not even paying attention to the fact that he is glowing blue. The second he gets ready to fire the fireball, he realizes that the environment around him changes. He sees that he is not in the ruined streets of the Magnus-ruins, but in a metal room. He sees everyone else in the room with him.

CHAPTER XII
Changing the Tide

Everyone is confused as they do not know where they are.

Jamie (annoyed): Where are we now?

Peter: Okay, the whole gang is here. Where is here?

Kylie: Wherever we are, it's not Earth.

Beth: What?

Intercom voice: Very astute observation, Agent Shulls. This is not Earth. Earth is the hellhole that we all used to reside in. Earth was the planet we called home. This is our new home now. This is the planet that the Onyx had created. This is the planet where we will plan to strike back against the Legion. This planet is...

Diane (excited): Oh my god! Jack, Antonio!!! They're actually here!

Jack: Diane?

Diane runs over to Jack and gives him a massive hug. Then Oz, Sparks, and Zack rush in excited to see everyone alive. Oz and Sparks go over to Jack and Antonio; Zack, not expect to see Beth, rushes to Kylie and Beth to gives them both a bearhug with enough strength to pick them both up.

Zack: Kylie! Beth!

Beth (excited): Zack! You're alive!

Bridgette: Oh come on, guys. I was getting in the moment here.

Tom: Bridgette, is that you?

Bridgette (disappointed): Yeah, it's me.

Tom: Commander, what's going on here?

Richard (relieved): We're out of the woods, Tom. We've been evacuated from Earth. We're finally safe, Tom.

Beth gets tired of the hug and then kicks Zack in the stomach to get him to let go of them. Zack drops Beth and Kylie and puts his hands on where she kicked him.

Zack (Acing): What the hell, Beth? The first time I see you in three years and you don't expect a bearhug from yours truly? This world has gone downhill.
Beth: Shut up, Zack. Can somebody please tell me where we are?
Richard: Who is this, Tom?
Tom: This is Beth, Commander. She's a friend of Kylie and Zack's. Kylie says she wants to join the Thunderbolts.

The doors to the Retrieval-Room open and they see Bridgette roll inside with her wheelchair. Everyone watches her roll in front of Tom and Richard. While watching Bridgette, Jack powers down to his normal state. However, his body is still effected by the Super-Pill. The enhances to his attributes were cut in half to have his attributes multiplier has been cut by half, his muscle mass goes back to normal, his hair turns back to normal, but the Golden Metal Headband is still on his head. This form is called Semi-Mode.

Bridgette (enthusiastically): Captain, Commander. I would love to welcome the two of you and everyone else to **Planet Onyx.**
Jamie: "Planet Onyx?"
Bridgette: Yes, you heard me right, mate. This is the most top secret file in the Onyx. A planet that the early Onyx actually created to be a fail-safe in case they would lose the Earth to any enemy.
Antonio: Well shit, that's convenient.
Peter: How come I have no data on this planet? There's nothing on my Ultranian data logs.
Bridgette: That's because they made it so that our planet could not be detected by any species in this universe. Not even the Ultranians.

Peter: How the fuck is that even possible?

Bridgette: Don't shoot the messenger, mate. That's all I know.

Jamie: How long have you known about this place?

Bridgette: Huh…?

Jamie: You know every single secret that the Onyx could hide and you would normally tell us any secret that they would have. Why didn't you tell us about this "planet" sooner? You would never let anything stop you before.

Bridgette (ashamed): Since the cat is out of the bag now. I found out about this place before we had that mission to find and capture the Ultranian King, you remember, a week before the Ultranians invaded Earth. I found these secret files and it revealed this planet to me and how it was created. McAllen found out the moment I hacked into it. He sent Agent Thomas to warm me that he'd kill me and everyone else in Omega-Squad if I told a single soul about this place.

Tom: Agent Thomas…

Sparks: Wait a second… tell me that I'm not the only one who's noticed that Jack looked like a Super Saiyan a minute ago.

Oz (amazed): He really did. Jack, how did you get this? The power I can sense in you is amazing.

Jack: Guys, there's something that I have to tell you all.

Bridgette: Hey, wait a minute. Where is everyone else?

Zack: That's what I was about to ask? Kylie, where's Kendall, Dom, and Sheila? I thought you went with Kendall to Mundi Castle.

Diane: Where's Gibson? Is he okay?

Zack sees Kylie look away with sadness in her eyes and Beth puts her hand on Zack's shoulder in order to get his attention.

Beth (sincere) Zack… I'm sorry.

Zack (confused): What are you talking about Beth?

Beth: Kendall… Kendall didn't make it.

Zack (state of denial): Wait… What did you just say?

Beth (remaining sincere): I said, "Kendall didn't make it."

Zack (laughing): You're playing with me, right Beth? Come on, this is Kendall we're talking about. He's incredibly powerful. He's like a young god. There no way he could die during all of this crap. Am I right?

He sees the uncharacteristic sincerity in Beth's eyes and realizes that she is not joking.

Zack: You're serious?
Beth (sincere): I wish I wasn't.
Zack: How did... how did he die?
Kylie: Dark-Knighten killed him. He tried to fight him by himself and his powers must've given up on him in the fight.
Zack (angry): What the fuck?! You went him to Mundi-Castle. So why the hell didn't you help my boy?!
Kylie (angry): I tried to help him, okay?! But, he used a darkness portal under my feet to send me to Denver before we were about to fight Dark-Knighten. I tried to help him and he just...
Zack: I'm having doubt that you tried hard enough.

Kylie, in a bit of blind fury, uppercut Zack in the chin so hard, she knock him off of his feet. This get Peter attention and he rushes to them.

Beth (startled): Hey, hey!
Zack (furious): Bitch, you must've lost your motherfucking mind!

Zack gets held back by Peter and Beth holds Kylie back to keep him from beating him more.

Zack: Peter, let me go!
Peter: Zack, calm down!
Kylie: "I didn't try hard enough?!" Did you really just say that, you asshole?! I tried the best I could've to convince him that he couldn't save Kenneth. He ignored everything I told him about it. He's been

wanting to save Kenneth from the very beginning. He would done anything if it meant saving Kenneth and there was nothing that any of us could've done to stop him! I tried, Zack!

Zack: Bitch, who are you trying to feel? You gave up on Kendall a long time ago!

Kylie: What do you mean?

Zack: We vowed to help each other out through good and bad times. You knew that what happened in that warehouse left mental scares on him because you found him there. He was hoping to have your help more than any of us because you promised to help him that day. But, you practically gave up on my boy and we all nearly died trying to help him without you.

Kylie: He was on the path Self-Ruin, you asshole. You nearly died to help his reckless path? You were encouraging his bad behavior. What was I supposed to do?

Zack: He was our friend. We risked our lives and reputations for each other all of the time because that's what friends are supposed to do. You just gave on him when he need us the most. Christina did more to help him than you did and she wasn't even the group for long at that point and she wasn't even that strong.

Beth: Zack…

Zack: You just stopped caring for him. You used to love the guy, but then you fell for Kyzo's ass and you threw his trust in you to the wolves.

Beth: Zack, Kylie… stop! Is arguing over going to bring him back? This won't get us anywhere!

Zack: What happened to Dom and Sheila?

Peter: We can't pick up their signals anywhere.

Kylie: And if you're wondering, we haven't the slightest idea where Christina is either.

Zack: Goddammit.

As Kylie and Beth tell Zack about Kendall, Sheila, and Dom, Jack tries to think of what to tell Oz, Antonio, Sparks, and Diane about Gibson. Jamie is looking at Jack to see how he is going to tell them.

Jamie knows that Jack has to tell them, no matter how much he does not want to.

Jack: Listen, I don't know how to tell all of you this. But… I went to Kinto to find Gibson and bring him to Magnus. But, the Legion got there before I did and somehow, they found out where he was and… they…
Oz: They what, Jack?
Antonio: Come on man, just tell us.
Jack: I'm sorry… Gibson didn't make it. By the time I found Gibson, he was already dead.

Every one of the Turbos go silent. Jack collapses on the ground on his knees after forcing himself to tell them the news. Diane gets on her knees and wails on the ground. Sparks gets on his knees to try to comfort his little sister, but he begins to cry too. Oz looks away and holds in his emotions in order to be strong about this, but it is hard for him to be strong. Antonio, however, is enraged and is not even trying to calm down.

Antonio (enraged): Somebody has to pay for this! Someone's going to fucking pay for this!
Oz: Calm down, Antonio. Now's not the time to lose out heads.

Antonio gets in Oz's face with a grin on his face.

Antonio: Don't you tell me to calm down. These motherfuckers are killing our families and friends and what are we supposed to, just fucking take it? Are we supposed to fucking take that shit? No! I'm not fucking taking that shit!

Oz incases Antonio in thick layers of ice with his ice-breath; Antonio cannot move.

Oz: No, you idiot. What we should do is not lose our minds so we don't end up joining them among the dead. Do you want to end up dead like Gibson?

Antonio (shivering): No.

Oz: Then calm down. Last thing we need is for you to act like your normal angry dumbass self.

Oz pokes Antonio's forehead and causes the ice to shatter; Antonio falls on his hands and knees, heavily breathing. Oz helps him up and right when he stands up right, Antonio punches Oz in the face. That unexpected punch puts Oz on the ground.

Antonio (serious): Fuck that shit! I'm not taking this shit any-goddamn-more. When Gordon killed out parents the day after Diane was born, we just took it. When he executed Maria in cold-blood in Kinto Central square, we just fucking took it. Now these Legion pieces of shit murdered Gibson and we're just going to fucking take it? Fuck that! I'm going to get Gordon's head on my wall the next time I see him.

Oz recovers off the ground and punches Antonio in the face in retaliation.

Oz: Why, you little…

Diane puts Oz and Antonio in force-fields to keep them from fighting each other and holds them up in the air.

Diane (tearful): Will you two shut up?

Everyone is at each other's throat. All, but Tom and Jamie after they tell Bridgette about Isabel and Tony and how Jacob is missing. Bridgette is able to cope with the news far better than the rest. But, Tom cannot even hear himself think.

Everyone then hears a loud gun-shot, creating a massive silence in the room and all eyes are on Tom and Jamie after Jamie shots at the ceiling with her sniper with sound suppression.

Tom: Zack... if you want to blame Kylie for Kendall's death, that's fine in the short-term. Antonio... if you're going to take your frustrations on your brothers and sister, that's fine in the short-term too. But, in the long-term, this is only going to make it easier for the Legion to divide us and hunt us down one by one. Yes, we have all lost someone important to us; we've lost Tony, Isabel, Kendall, and Gibson; we more likely lost Jacob, Sheila, and Dom too. And what are we doing here; we're just arguing at each other, making excuses, and placing blame on someone else. We're on the brink of losing this war and we're fighting each other. All of them, all of us were in this fight and they knew the risks as well as we know that fighting over them will not bring any of them back. We'll all join them in the afterlife if we keep fighting each other instead of fighting the enemy, and that's assuming if there is one. But, if this war is taking too much of a toll on all of you and you do not want to fight, then that is perfectly fine too. So here and now, I'm giving all of you a choice, you can stay and fight against the Legion or you can give up and we will send you back to Earth and cut all ties to us and you'll be on your own. That goes for all of you. Stay and fight or leave?

Tom has put a lot of emotion into that speech. All of the Thunderbolts look at each other and they see that nobody is choosing to leave. All of the Thunderbolts know that they have gone too far to turn back new and they also know there is nothing to turn back to. Each of them know that they cannot give on the fight and the people they have lost in the past and they all chose to stay and fight. They all begin to stand bold and tall. Peter goes to get Agent Thomas out of the recked Omega-Star and goes next to Tom.

Peter: Captain, I think I can speak for everyone here when I say, We're all Thunderbolts and we're all going to fight until the very end. No second earlier.

Tom: Is Peter right?

Jamie: As always. We didn't come this far to give up.

Jack: I told you that I would stay and fight.

Zack: Those Legion scumbags are going to pay for what they've done to all of us.

Beth: I may be new to this Thunderbolt thing, but I'm not going to crawl and hide like a cowardly little bitch. I owe that to my friends.

Sparks: We're all in this together. For all of the people who died in the war and the people who can still make it.

Richard: The Thunderbolts are far more than a military unit. We are all a family and we will stand as such. Together. Even if we will all die together. We are the Onyx.

Bridgette: We are the Thunderbolts. Am I right, team?

Thunderbolts: Oorah!

Tom (impressed): <Sob> Alright then. Let's get going. We have a new world to see.

The Thunderbolts walk out of the retrieval-room; Jamie wheels Bridgette out. Zack walks out with his arms wrapped around Kylie and Beth's shoulders to show that they are still close. Diane helps Jack up off the ground, letting Jack know that she will be strong from now on and the Turbos follow them all. They all walk out to the retrieval balcony to look at the sky of the city of New-Magnus in Planet Onyx. They see the purple night sky; billions of stars are glowing bright in the sky; the beauty of the cosmos shines over them; there is zero light pollution from city lights. They are all mesmerized at the sight of the sky. Bridgette reaches out for Tom's hand and grabs it; getting his attention.

Bridgette: It's beautiful, isn't it Tom?

Tom: It's incredible. I never thought I'd live to see anything like it.

Antonio: It's like when I first tasted Chipotle.

Oz: That's exactly what Zack said when we first saw the view.

Zack (tearful): And I meant it. I wish all of us were here to see this though.

Kylie puts her hand on Zack's shoulder to comfort him.

Kylie: I'm sure they're all in a better place now.
Zack: Yeah, I know. I'm sorry for being an ass back there, Kylie.

Kylie goes silent as she knows that there was a bit of truth to Zack's words.

Jamie sees that Jack is still saddened about Gibson; she leans on him to comfort him as he is going another real dark time in his life. Jack appreciate Jamie being there for him; he wraps his arm around her shoulder.

Diane grows jealous due to how she can't see the sky as she is blind.

Diane (jealous): You guys are making jealous right now. You know I can't see the sky.

A carrier jet hovers in front of the balcony to pick them all up and take them. It opens and three Hail-Guards greet Richard.

Hail-Guard: Generalissimo Sullivan. The High-Council is waiting for you in the Plaza. For you and Captain Sullivan.
Richard: Understood. Alright, Thunderbolts… we have a lot of work to do.

The Thunderbolts board the carrier jet and it flies towards the plaza.

All of them believe that they are safe and finally have a safe-haven after going into the flames of war and coming out on the losing side, but they are unaware that they were being watched the second they were teleported to the planet.

???: The Thunderbolts are more resourceful than any of us ever thought. I thought you said that the Legion would destroy them.

???: 20-8-3 7-3-14-3-18-1-12-9-19-19-9-13-15 1-9-4-3-4 20-8-5-13. 9 20-15-12-4 25-15-21 20-8-3 3-15-21-14-3-9-12 23-1-19 19-16-9-14-5-12-5-19-19.

???: Yeah, but so are the rest of the Onyx. Those kids are more dangerous than they look. Guess we have to kill them first before we even think about initiating the plan.

???: 1-7-18-5-5-4. 3-15-14-20-1-3-20 20-8-5 1-7-1-20-5 1-7-5-14-20-19. 20-8-9-19 23-1-18 9-19 19-20-1-18-20-9-14-7 1-8-5-1-4 15-6 19-3-8-5-4-21-12-5.

??? *Chuckles* This is gonna be fun.

???: 18-5-13-5-13-2-5-18, 9-6 1-14-25-15-14-5 11-9-12-12-19 19-21-12-12-9-22-1-14, 9-20 23-9-12-12 2-5 13-5.

???: Which one again…? You know there's two of them, right?

???: 20-15-13, 25-15-21 9-4-9-15-20.

???: Ooooooh! I knew that…

<u>Next time: Bleeding Secrets</u>

Printed in the United States
By Bookmasters